FLUTTER BRAND©

BOOK Five
of the
SECRET BUTTERFLY SERIES™

A Novel by

Rosemary Lightfoot Ness-Bitner

This book is dedicated to lovers and their dreams.

The eBook and print version layouts of BUTTERFLY CONFIDES were done by Andrea Reider; the cover was created by Cheeky Covers; and I am Melanie Monarch, your audio book narrator.

Hello, dear readers and listeners, in our fourth book, BUTTER-FLY CONFIDES, of THE SECRET BUTTERFLY (tm) SERIES, we learned how Marty feels about making explicit erotica films. We met her new coach, Bertie, and her husband, George. We heard how intensely emotional Marty feels about Marshawn, one of her performing partners. Is Marty in love or merely acting? How can we tell the difference? She expresses her feelings about Josh, another performer she holds deep affections for in FLUTTTER BRAND, this fifth book of our series. But, is what Marty feeling truly love, or are these feelings merely nymphomania disguised as love? Does Marty know the difference? George and Bertie are both falling into love with Marty. Where will their new obsession take them? Let's get our answers and let's find out if Marty is getting closer to discovering true love. Come flutter with me, Melanie Monarch, as I narrate FLUTTER BRAND, the fifth book of THE SECRET BUTTERFLY (tm) SERIES.

CHAPTER ONE

For a man, he must go with a woman, which women don't understand; or the sort that say they can see it, they aren't the marrying brand. (Rudyard Kipling: The Mary Gloster)

What is it about our porn stars? Why do they fascinate us; make us wonder about them, and ourselves? Is it the salacious deeds they perform? Their bodies? Their casualness about peccadillos and depravity? Four yeses; but even more are the workings of their minds. Are they different from other women; or, like them, all fine martinis; but with added drops of spicey bitters and tarty twists of lime? (Rosemary Ness-Bitner: Author)

THE MARTY BRAND

"A brand?" George's puzzled look said it all. He understood beer and auto brands, but branding a woman? Bertie's declaration gave him mental whiplash. His mind was already fractured between limbic lust for Marty and rational thought. A 'Marty Brand!' The mere thought overloaded his brain. It crashed. He wanted to make love with Marty, not talk about making her a household brand name.

"Yes, George, a BRAND! Like a beer company has a brand image, or a dish detergent has a brand image. A brand, George. We are going to painstakingly brand the one emotion that most satisfies the need for escapism. We're going to brand love. People need a mental respite from the chaos and disorder in their world. They

are frustrated with the dual standards and corruptions that they can't do anything about. They want to turn off cognitive thought and switch on self-gratifying, limbic thought.

"They want to escape stress. Pornography is the answer for many, George; but it's a fragmented, hodge-podge industry. We'll rebrand pornography as 'Intimate Artistry.' We'll market it as attainable, empathetic freedom; fantastical love with beautiful, glorious, explicit romantic sex. Marty's breathtaking, uninhibited erotic immorality will be our brand. Our iconic logo will be her eyes behind her spellbinding vagina's butterfly wings. 'EYES BEHIND THE BUTTERFLY,'™ will symbolize the freedom portal every soul needs. Its eyes will welcome escapees; promise freedom from responsibility and stress. 'Leave your cares; discover romantic, erotic love.' will be Marty's message.

"We'll use film, print and billboard advertising to carry her message. We'll market Marty as the Superstar of Intimacy; Goddess of Love; and Queen of Promiscuity. We'll hail her as World's Greatest Intimate Artisan; most accomplished artisan of erotic intimacy. We'll position her billboard marquee figure atop imagery of sensuality and romance. She'll have the best cosmetics, artfully applied; and the finest, most erotic outfits. She'll never wear the same outfit twice. Her hair will always be perfectly coifed; her nails perfectly filed, trimmed, and painted; her lingerie will be shimmering, transparent silk lace; stimulating, new, and provocative. She'll be the world's living poster girl for erotic romantic love.

"Her image will be daring, bold and conscious-free about her immorality; earning revile from religious types and prudes; while always advancing her brand. Aficionados of explicit intimate art will consider her their angelic cherub. They will adore her. We'll get testimonials from her performing partners about her wonders. We'll get media coverage that drools over every thought she has and every word she speaks. She'll be the personification of incorrigible,

wanton sin. Red blooded mortals will pine for her; and they will love her! Everyone seeking passion's lusts will revel in her still photos and films."

George rolled his eyes, then stared dumbfounded at Bertie's babbling. His limbic mind wanted to stop her shop talk and free his penis to fornicate. *"Bertie, Marty's a whore, a porn star! How are we going to brand something that happens in every barnyard?"* George's rational mind tried to contribute to objectivity. His attempt was halfhearted. He offered no other alternatives. Limbic domination prevented his mind from thinking deeply. And Bertie doomed his objection to fall flat. She wasn't having it.

"George, listen to me. I've always been smarter than you, right?"

"Right, but........." George hesitated, unsure of who his wife had become or what he could say. And pushing hard against his consciousness was his overpowering desire to copulate with Marty. He intuitively knew the vixen loved Bertie's commitment to her; but would also welcome a reprieve from Bertie's lecturing. Her eyes had already signaled that she wanted sex as much as he did; if only Bertie would stop pontificating about her business plan, and leave them to their inclinations. But Bertie wasn't about to leave the film room. When Bertie had an idea, she chewed on it.

"No buts, George, listen. Everyone who understands propaganda understands this one critical fact about humans: People do not like to think for themselves. Their minds are naturally lazy. Thinking for oneself requires hard work. Most people naturally hate hard work. They want someone to tell them what to think. They look for that someone to lead them about by the nose, the same way we lead horses.

"If they are told they'll be happier and safer if I kill someone who poses a threat to their comfort, they'll go along with it. They won't even bother thinking that killing someone is wrong; especially when they are told it's a great idea and it's for a good reason. They won't

stop to think ahead that, by agreeing to kill someone, they could be next. Their minds are that lazy, George."

"So..............?" George's mind was reeling. Was Bertie prattling on like this to keep him from Marty? He could only wonder.

"So," Bertie cut off his thought," *if they can be convinced that cigarettes and alcohol are good for them; if they can be convinced that watching nonstop violence in theaters and on television is good for them; then, they can be convinced to believe anything and every- thing else! If they get some reward to go along with what they are being told, they'll agree with what they are told. They'll believe when the government tells them black is white; up is down; left is right; loss of freedom is good; hating someone with a different skin color is desirable; and wars makes you safe. Get it?"*

"Okay, I get that, but what do we give them, and how are you going to......................?" For George, maintaining this thought track was like having a tooth pulled. His penis desperately wanted to be inside Marty's vagina. His mind now agreed with his penis, but Bertie was on a roll. She wasn't about to let George leave her discussion.

"*We give them PERMISSION, George. We tell them that it's okay to watch the porn they already love watching secretly. Our mes- saging will make watching porn acceptable; even desirable and chic. We'll fashion our message to make people agree that porn isn't even porn anymore. We'll make them see it as an art form that's evolved. We'll convince them it has morphed into intimate artistry. And, by becoming intimate artistry, it is now, in its changed form, completely respectable. It will be Avant Garde.*

"*We'll give their minds permission to call prostitution ser- vices and have liaisons with sex workers. Our brand marketing will convince viewers that prostitution services are naturally healthy outlets that are necessary for relieving their stresses; and that their consorting trysts with prostitutes are perfectly normal, healthy activities. Subscribing to our branded films and buying our branded erotica merchandise will become viewed as psychologically healthy, novel, and chichi. We'll give their minds all the excuses they need to do what they already crave doing. And we'll give them the permissions that they were always afraid to request. We'll tell them it's now acceptable and desirable to think objectively about their religious beliefs. We'll make it acceptable and modern for people to challenge their moral teachings; and reject them. We'll open their eyes to the immediate benefits of worshiping Marty's immorality brand instead."*

"What benefits?" George hoped his skepticism would corral Bertie's babble. Maybe then he could get Marty away from the film room and make love with her, out of sight from his wife. Dared he hope?

Bertie didn't relent. She continued her enthusiastic charge. *"Well, George, freedom from stress and guilt for starters. And freedom from responsibility, and your right to choose whom you make love with; and for how long. Face it, George, permanent relationships are extremely rare in the animal kingdom. They aren't natural. Just look at the two of us, George. Look where our marriage is and where we are headed with Marty.*

"People will accept Marty's Modern Morality Standard. They benefit from it and no one gets hurt by it. There is no harm in it, unless a person is terribly possessive and close-minded. Listen to me, George! What I plan to do with our brand building is not any different than cigarette advertizing. We create this image: That people who are attracted to Marty's intimate artistry are in charge of their life's decisions; that they are people who are adult enough to think for themselves; that they are making a mentally healthy decision for themselves when they surrender their souls and their money to Marty; and that they are too mature to accept the ridiculous constraints of some institution's moral authority."

"But I can foresee where our glorification of Marty's pornography could cause problems." George decided to challenge Bertie's assertion that only good could come of their involvement with Marty. He implied that their relationship with her would only fuel Marty's nympho narcissism, taking them into unchartered psychological waters.

"For instance?" Bertie shot back. George's caution was simple enough, but she wasn't having it. Her eyes dared George to defy her perfect scenario. George cleared his throat before he addressed his wife's skepticism:

WHO'S TO BLAME?

Faultless to a fault! (Robert Browning: The ring and the book)

Can anyone honestly blame a girl who can't say no? (Rosemary Ness-Bitner: Author)

George began his reply:

"Well, let's say a man becomes addicted to Marty's film art. He joins her premium Service without telling his wife. One night he's in his home's office, thinking he has privacy. He's troubled. He feels compelled to see one of Marty's films, but he doesn't know his wife is spying on him. The wife is a church mouse. She's forbidden the husband from seeing Marty's films. He chooses to disobey the wife and watches the film. There's a scene where Marty makes love with a man seated in a large leather chair. I'm imagining he's watching that sensational film she made with Marshawn. Her leg is draped over the arm of the chair; she's kissing Marshawn while he fondles her breasts and plies her vagina with his penis.

"Our male viewer's rapture lust for Marty builds and builds while he watches the scene. What captivates his imagination is that Marty is obviously, thoroughly enjoying herself. She's laughing, giggling, and teasing Marshawn while they are making love. It's not

work for her. Marty's having a fabulous time. She's completely carefree and guiltless in her immoral revelry. The man can not reconcile this in his cognitive mind. Here is a woman making passionate love with a man who plays the role of a perfect stranger; and she thoroughly loves what she's doing. He reflects upon his own life. He thinks of himself as a 'yes' man; mere cog in some corporate wheel; a human sock puppet; and a man beholden to his wife; a coward in his own home! He asks himself: 'Dare I cavort with Marty, as this man is doing? Would Marty have me?' George was on one of his imagination rides. Bertie and Marty listened while George's script played itself out:

"Our film performers are not committed to each other in the ordinary sense. They are not raising a family or engaged in some common purpose together. Their love making is, in itself, the sum total of their erotic romance. The whole purpose of their union is divinely simple. It is to wantonly fornicate and behave in a debauched immoral way, for the sheer joy of it. Their wanton act of carnal love making is the beautiful mystery that binds these two partners together in their erotic romance. Nothing else; nothing more. It's not more complicated than that. There is no intricate plot. They have no common goal. Making love to slake their libidos' physical attractions is the entire plot goal. Our viewer man understands this. He realizes the film is divinely beautiful in its honest simplicity."

George's eyes gauged Marty's and Bertie's interest in his scenario. They were both paying close attention. He continued:

"Our viewer focuses on Marty's Vagina. It reveals her lover has ejaculated. The filtered stage lights play their magical effects. Marty's widespread legs reveal rivulets of Marshawn's semen. Alternating tints of white, pink, and orange artistically display her semen flows over the glowing sheen of her glossily waxed vagina. The flows glisten as they spill from her triumphant inner vaginal lips. Our viewer is mesmerized. He's overwhelmed by the film's explicit eroticism and

Marty's carefree, casual sinfulness. The cameras close in. They high-light the semen flow and spattered semen on Marty's inner lips. Her warm, enthusiastic smile signals that she is extremely proud of her carnal deed; delighted that she has successfully brought Marshawn to ejaculation inside of her. The scene is breathtakingly artistic. It plays on and haunts our viewer's mind. Marty's vaginal lips resemble the seductive invitational markings splattered on the insides of an orchid flower's pink-taupe petals. Like the orchid's flower, Marty's vagina is an irresistible invitation to partake in endless, wanton sexual nirvana.

"In each hand Marty now holds a freshly hardened penis. Her joyous smile signals our distraught, viewing wife that Marty's shameless revelry has only just begun. As Marty brings one of these cocks to her mouth, she coos her adoration messages to it and begins kissing it, while two more lovers bring bouquets of red roses to her, kissing her toes while they lay their flowers before her, glorifying her wanton promiscuity. Marty's iniquity, her abandonment of morality is symbolically honored by their rose offerings. The messaging which the film imparts to its viewers is that immorality is wonderous, glorious, and holy; and, counterintuitively, that Marty's shameless, sinful whoring is miraculous and divine. The viewing wife's sense of what a woman's acceptable conduct should be has now been stood on its head. She is reeling in her discomfort."

George made his point very well. He sent Bertie's imagination into overdrive. He paid close attention to Bertie's sense of the scene he narrated. His penis stayed rock hard; hopeful; anticipating its introductory moment with Marty. Bertie and Marty listened to George's continuing narration:

"The watching wife is horrified. Her mind suffers an incomprehensible jolt. She observes her husband. He's succumbing to a whore's blasphemy! In our film, Marty is performing a subtle type of pantomime. Her lurid lines mock the Savior's arrival in Jerusalem

on his mission to save the world. Marty's message is the opposite of the scriptures' passages. Marty's imagery implies that, to save the world, one must procreate, not die on a cross. Her followers must honor the resurrecting, stress-healing powers, and human rebirthing powers of the female vagina; not the redemptive soul resurrecting powers of the Savior."

Bertie's eyebrows lifted. She looked at George, impressed with where his tale was taking them. George continued:

"Marty's film confronts the religious wife with an explicit in-your-face challenge. It openly opposes the wife's view of religion and morality. In our film, Marty positioned herself upon a raised platform under a canopy fashioned as the holy apse. Her lovers ascended seven broad steps to reach her; and they laid roses at her feet! Was this imagery not meant to imply that our lovely Marty's vagina was the Holy of Holies for the New Modern Morality Standard? Were those ejaculations her partners spurted onto her tongue not meant to symbolize that she was receiving the bodily commitment hosts from her immoral followers, instead of the traditional dispensing of a host wafer into mouths of religious congregants?

"You see, Bertie, our film challenges the religious view that the spiritual path to eternal life is gained by paying homage to death. Our work contends that the true spiritual path to eternal life is through the celebration of life. The wife's mind suffers whiplash. It races crazily. It acknowledges that honoring life is greatly preferred to honoring death. But this presents her with an impossible conundrum. It struggles to reconcile these opposing views; but finds nothing that consoles it. Appreciating this opposing, different reality for the first time in her life, causes the wife impossible stress and consternation. She fears her husband will lose his way and his faith. The film causes her deep distress."

Bertie and Marty exchange looks. Both women wonder how George's hypothetical story will end. George noted that he held his audience of two in the palm of his hand. Marty affirmed her attentiveness by placing her hand upon George's cock. His enthusiasm for his penis's situation brought excitement to his voice:

"Our viewing husband stops the film. He replays Marty's mesmerizing fornication scene several times; then he sits in a semi-conscious dream state. He memorizes and memorializes the explicit, erotic scene for long moments. He has watched earlier films of Marty's erotica. Afterwards he was able to close his mind's door to her scenes and go about his business and his life. But he has now returned to watch her films again and again. He believed he controlled a manageable condition. But he is sliding into addiction to Marty's porn.

"And this film was different from all that preceded it. It was the first one we produced where we applied Bertie's coaching techniques and her flare for visual dramatization. This is the film that powered Marty's fast climb in her porn star rankings. It is an exceptional work of art. Millions of men, myself included, fell in love with Marty while watching it. Its genius lifts Marty above the ceiling that previously held down pornography. Marty transcended that unspoken boundary. She left the constraints that held other porn stars to the conventional beliefs on planetary Earth. She soared above all of them. Marty defeated gravity.

"Bertie's genius use of high vertical plane doors to introduce the viewers to Marty's boudoir; her clever, subtle introduction of chiaroscuro light shading and blending, combined with diagonal, angular set walls and focused soft illumination effects playing over Marty's body, drew the viewers' eyes directly to Marty. Bertie's set scheme and lighting accentuated the message that everything in the room was subservient to our glorious sex-minx; nothing else mattered compared with the pleasures-seeking of our gorgeous woman-child. Bertie had judiciously placed a tiara on Marty's head and purple satin pillows on the royal bed scene,

including a very large one under Marty's tush. Kudos, Bertie. Your added touches magnified Marty's magnificence. They convinced our viewer that she is intimacy's goddess exemplar! Queen sex symbol of the world!

"Our royal queen of intimacy, here; this gorgeous sex bunny sitting beside me, captivated her viewers in this film while dispensing her sexual favors to her favored subjects under Bertie's brilliantly crafted, intimate lighting scheme. The focused close ups of her vagina's explicit copulations with her partners imaged her butterfly tattoo as heavenly angel's wings, ushering those who sought refuge from life's turmoil and corruption into her intimate sanctuary. There, these souls discovered their new, understanding and accepting world. There, they experienced redemption and affirmation of who they were as mortal men. To her welcoming sanctuary these men brought their troubles, their failings, their inadequacies, and their indecisiveness. Inside her sanctuary, during intimacy with her, they discovered the acceptance they craved, and the forgiveness they needed to live and the peace they needed to resurrect their souls.

"As the white semen rivulets of those souls' salvations flowed from Marty's sanctuary onto the purple satin pillow, the film created the indelible imagery of sweet innocence taking its deserved repose. Each innocent soul communed. It received acceptance into Marty's forgiving, loving world. Now its life force flowed into the purple sea below her glorious sin-temple, joining its very soul to her peacefully dark, immoral world. In the semen rivulets' new world, sin as humanity understood it before, ceased to exist. It disappeared, leaving only the glory of love and the honest appreciation of erotic pleasures, as the purple satin received the soul cleansing flows.

"Bertie, your imagery messaging was brilliant; breathtaking. The dramatization effects of the film's erotic scenes made Marty's explicitly, ravishing fornications unforgettable. You captured her passion and energy beautifully. She took my breath away. All

viewers, like myself, could, from those scenes onward, only imag-
ine Marty as a saintly, divinely inspired, woman; a personage of
unlimited, sincere, loving goodness; a woman who could never,
under any circumstances, betray the trust of any of her lovers; a
woman they could confidently love and adore. You two created
the most memorable image of innocent immorality ever filmed
before those moments. You created spectacular intimate artistry.
Congratulations!

"That film's scenes and choreography were brilliant; flawlessly
performed. Now, viewers can no longer shove Marty's performance
into mental closets for viewing later at their convenience. Explicit
images of Marty's joyful copulations became indelibly stamped into
the prurient minds of every single viewer. They salivated. I know they
did. I was in a theater watching them. There is no such thing as too
much Marty for the people who watched that film. They want more
of her. Marty's intimacy suddenly filled a societal vacuum. People
couldn't get enough of her. Viewers saw enlarged visual enhance-
ments of Marty's wax-sheen butterfly wings and glossy vaginal lips
occupying the entire screen during her most explicit, erotic moments.
Her sensual orifices literally reached out from the film set, enveloped
our viewers' erotic imaginations, and captured their prurient souls.
You bonded Marty's intimacy to viewers' hearts. They welcomed her
as their true goddess of intimacy. She swept away every porn star
they ever idolized previously.

"Bertie's genius close-up effects; the pulsing, colored light filters,
and Marty's sensuous acting suddenly made intimacy with her seem
possible; attainable and irresistible. All who saw that film wanted
more; more Marty; more Marty performing her exquisite, explicitly
delicious, mouthwatering intimate artistry.

"But now, let's return to our particular viewing man. He is pos-
itively, hopelessly smitten by Marty's sexually explicit nirvana. His

lusts burst limbic containment. He's become fixated. He's experiencing a transformational event. He wants Marty. He loves her.

"He obsesses over the film's most explicit erotica scenes. They are exquisitely presented in slow motion frames that, thanks to Bertie's creativity, allow the viewer to visualize, frame by frame, the pulsations and contractions of every penis that ejaculates spurts of semen into Marty's mouth and vagina. Bertie's production skills make the film a breathtaking, unforgettable work of intimate artistry. The eroticism of the film becomes plausibly tangible to our viewer. He imagines Marty is there, in his study, beside him. She performs her exquisite fellatio with his penis; and she makes love with him in his imaginary real time and space. He relishes all of it. Our winsome minx seems tangible, real, touchable, and possibly his. She's beautiful, spellbinding, and glorious. He's beyond smitten. She is irresistible. His love for her takes him to obsession's precipice of madness. There's a compelling divine holiness about Bertie's new intimacy artistry stylizing that makes our viewer desire to surrender his life and soul to Marty. This is a new, compelling phenomena. His transformed mind worships Marty. She becomes his goddess.

"His worship state ensconces a liberation effect in his mind. Marty's entrancing erotic effect can never be dislodged. He must honor it. Firmly planted, it grows like a weed. It strangle-chokes all thoughts of his wife; mentally killing her. Meanwhile, Bertie's production film rolls forward. It reaches the segment where Marty's smiles over her ejaculation successes are still-framed; magnified and moved forward slowly, one frame at a time. Bertie has brilliantly captured in Marty's face, her spectacular, deeply emotive feelings. The film frames emphasize the unbridled joy Marty feels while she revels in her lovemaking.

"The camera captures Marty's eyes, wearing her gleam-sheen of pleasuring's satisfaction. As each consorting penis spurts its fresh *offerings onto her receptive lips and into her insatiable vagina, her eyes radiate glory; the incomparable majesty of her shameless iniquity. Each still frame enlarges to full screen. Sensational! Remarkable! Indelible, magnificent intimacy! You created it, Bertie! You performed it, Marty! Bravo to both of you! Marty's film face is now transformed to an unforgettable life-like presence. Those frames subtly beckoned our viewer to bind his feelings to Marty's expressively shameless, immoral innocence; and to hold her face in his hands and kiss her inviting lips. The film's effect causes our viewer's mind to acquiesce to Bertie's view; that immorality is normal and wholesome and good.*

"The erotic weed next wraps its eros around our viewer's mind and takes control of it. His limbic mind assures him that it's normal and moral to obey the weed's craving. It wants to meet Marty, the real, in-the-flesh, Marty. It wants to hold her in its arms; place her on its lap; kiss her; fondle her breasts; make immoral sinful love with her. It wants to place its thirsting tongue into the same place where it saw the pink taupe-like vagina's orchid-like white semen spots and streaks. And, it wants his penis to enter his dream vagina-orchid's love channel, immersing it within Marty's velvety heaven; never to come out again.

"His mind no longer sees his wife as a desirable companion asset. His romantic attachment to her has passed its expiration date. He imagines his new lap doll wants his undivided devotion. His mind mentally pleases Marty; imagining taking his wife to the curb, setting her beside the trash; her usefulness spent. His mind is all in, for Marty. All that's left to do is command his body to follow through.

"Meanwhile, Marty's eyes express her honest beliefs that her performance is pure goodness and sincerity. The viewer knows he is witnessing honesty. Obviously, our nymph goddess believes

wholeheartedly in the righteousness of her immoral performance. Our viewer obeys his natural instincts to pursue his beguiling goddess. He follows his mind's desire; becomes a willing convert to Marty's charms. He silently applauds her victory over his morality; forsakes it, and pursues her divinely unapologetic immorality. He believes everything Marty represents is right; and everything he ever learned in church was a horrific mistake.

"Our film is more compelling than anything that came before it. It rivets our man's attention. He can not close his mind's door on this film like he did Marty's pre-Bertie films. The scenes in this film haunt him relentlessly, constantly. They flood his limbic senses, searching out and flooding every nook and cranny of his mind. They consume him, immersing him in imaginary visions. All his resistances to Marty's wanton culture exhaust themselves. They capitulate, surrender, and bow to her confident, goddess-like iniquity. The man imagines holding Marty in his arms; kissing her affectionately. He craves being with her to confess his adoration. He becomes a smitten schoolboy, consumed with obsessive infatuation over his first love."

George's eyes melted into Marty's. He identified, personally, with the hypothetical man in his narrative. He never, in all his life, yearned to make love with a woman as badly as he now yearned to make love with Marty. He could not take his eyes off her as he continued describing his imaginary scene:

"His breath is stolen away while he watches in wonderment, as Marty fornicates with lover after lover. He's spellbound by the joy with which she takes penis after penis into her hands, brings them to her irresistible lips and kisses them before receiving them into her mouth. He's awestruck by the homage her lovers pay to her, by laying bouquet after bouquet of red roses at her feet; and by how they humbly kiss her toes after doing so."

George imagined himself in the scene now. His eyes contin-ued melting longingly into Marty's. His own narration had him so hard it was all he could do to not push Marty back onto the bed and roll onto her. That thought was there, but, courageously, he restrained himself. He continued, nearly breathless: *"Our viewer's dream of making love with Marty stays with him. It haunts his every thought. It builds and builds until he can no longer place it into some context within his rational mind. The film is no longer enough. His erogenous senses are accosted and overwhelmed by the indelible frame-by- frame images of semen flows from Marty's vaginal lips; and ejaculating semen flows from penis after penis onto her smil-ing, welcoming lips and into her mirthful mouth. These scenes create unforgettable explicit images; seared forever into his memory. He has yet to touch or hold Marty in his arms, or kiss her. But despite their physical distancing, he's certain he loves her.*

"His limbic mind knows that Marty is his true path to happi-ness and eternal life. He believes making love with her will release him from all his tensions and insecurities. He's enraptured with his thoughts; consumed with dreams of making love with Marty. He fantasizes that the penis he witnessed ejaculating into her vagina was his. He dreams fervently that the next penis she ardently cud-dles, mouths and sucks will be his, for real; that the testicles she mouths and caresses will be his, as well. She's ethereal, mystical. She enchants and transforms. She is an invasive species weed, growing rampantly in his mind.

"His entire life dissipates. It is a fog lifting. His soul slips away from reality; binds with and combines with Marty's soul. Her film artistry absorbs his very soul. The genius of our work magnifies Marty's allure to this hapless bloke. Bertie's shadow art, played in slow motion, arrests his imagination. His mind explodes with lust. He sees screen shadows of penises transiting Marty's breasts on their sojourn to her sanctuary vagina. He salivates. Silhouettes of her

face, mouthing shadow images of penis after penis, play alternately in titillating film frames, between unforgettable scenes of her deliciously immoral fellatio. The film's creativity, and Marty's delightfully immoral imagery, bludgeon our bloke's cognitive mind. His raging limbic thirst must be quelled. He submits.

"He must have Marty. The man within him cries out his need. He must partake of Marty's glorious, unrepentant sinfulness. His lusts cannot accept denial. She has become his beautiful dream goddess; reincarnated, irresistible divine temple goddess; glorious Goddess Ishtara, come to him from ten thousand years ago; eager to love him; willing to dispel all his troubles; absolve him of every care and guilt.

"He embarks upon a mental journey that has no return. He knows he can't dislodge the images of Marty's erotic lovemaking from his mind. Trying to fight the effect she has on his mind is useless. His cognitive mind fully understands that he will never have an actual future life with Marty. He knows that he is only one among millions of men who desire to consort with her. His thinking brain even understands that consorting with her will, undoubtedly, upend his world; destroy everything he has built over his entire lifetime. He intuits that placing a call to Marty's Premium Member Service will sentence his marriage to its death. He knows the call will create, at least, a year of miserable divorce turmoil.

"But, hey! He's a guy, isn't he? Naturally, he thinks like a guy thinks. He believes that he is something special. He believes he can take the inside track for a life with Marty! He is delusional; but that's what being a guy is all about, isn't it? There's that limbic zone component of his mind. It flushes rational thought down the drain. It dominates his actions. It throbs with lust for our insatiable siren. He's powerless to contain or silence his raging lust. It has reached rampage state. His blood pulses with desire for our glorious goddess. His blood lust becomes a raging madman, caged and outraged at its confinement. It yearns to be set free. It demands he act. It builds

in strength and momentum. It rattles the cage it's in. And it roars at him from its rage state: 'Let me have her. Give her to me! I must have her!'

"It silently screams and morphs. It's a Tsunami wave that sweeps over his entire reason for being a man. Steadily his mountain wave rises until it overwhelms and drowns all his other motivations for living. This limbic sensation is different from the stirrings he gets from inspiring music. Those leave him when he steps outside the concert hall or the church. Those he can manage.

"But this limbic effect is different. It's primal. It does not leave when he turns off the video. It builds and builds. It haunts; entwines his heart. Unlike the concert hall or church, its calling becomes stronger when he's away from it. It intensifies; beckons; produces aching cravings in his stomach; makes his heart race faster. It commands him to act; drop all resistance to it; succumb; slake it, no matter the cost or the pain it causes. It controls. Unlike other stirrings, it commands him to obey. It becomes his new God. Marty awakened it. It addicts him. He cannot know peace unless he follows its command to go to Marty; join God to Goddess; copulate. It is a command he cannot refuse."

Marty listened attentively. She loved George's imagery. Repeatedly, she softly squeezed and relaxed her grip on George's penis. She, too, was captivated. George took her hand in his. She squeezed it. Her deep eye pools melted into George's eyes. They signaled that she wanted him. The two of them stared starry-eyed into each other's eyes; there, right in front of Bertie. Marty took her hand back and reasserted her grasp on George's penis, as if declaring that it, and George, were hers. Slowly, confidently, heedless of Bertie's possible jealousy, she stroked and squeezed it while George returned to his narration:

"Like a moth to a flame, our viewer's limbic thoughts compel him onward. He'll eagerly embrace his fate on whatever terms Marty

offers. His lust rage is overpowering. He'll give Marty whatever she demands to lie with her just one precious, unforgettable time. He can not resist her for another second.

"His rational mind next capitulates to Marty's allure. It the neighboring domino to the limbic mind which already fell. Now, it also falls. Our man reasons: even if his adventure leads to divorce, that will not end his world. There will be life after his wife. He'll still occasionally see his children. He'll still make money and have a place to live. Best of all, he'll be free to see Marty. He won't need to make excuses about why he's been away. He won't need to sneak around. His only constraints will be Marty's availability and her price.

"He ponders how two women could possibly be so different. His wife resists sex, and often resents it afterwards. Her behavior is the product of the reference frame that raised her. Marty's behavior is the product of the reference frame she created for herself. Two behaviors; irreconcilably opposite.

"He rationalizes that he has lived in the wrong life's reference frame his entire life. He now accepts that reasoning; agrees to it, and changes his life. He willfully blinds himself to all change's consequences. He's a guy, right? He'll deal with consequences later. He whole heartedly wants Marty. His limbic mind and rational mind join forces. They are of one accord. Bedding Marty becomes his absolute, singular goal, even if she will only see him for an hour. He's now willing to give over his very life to our screen goddess. He'll do anything to please her. He loves her unapologetic immorality, unconditionally. He holds Marty's debauched behaviors in awe, fully accepting her immoral ways and her pronouncements about the rightness of her views. Capitulation happens. He becomes Marty's adoring convert. There's zero consequential thought involved in this decision. He's a guy, remember?

"His adoration further transforms him. He becomes Marty's worshiper. Marty is his divine goddess; his new religion. He willfully surrenders his life to her New Modern Morality cause. He becomes her faithful disciple.

"He visualizes his life's purpose anew. It is to ejaculate his seed into Marty, thereby expressing the surrender of his life and soul to her. He knows he can not impregnate her. Like the temple prostitutes of thousands of years before her, Marty practices contraception. He intends for his ejaculation offerings to nevertheless pay tribute to her; surrender his will to hers and thusly honor her and her irrepressible sexuality, much as ancient pagan worshipers paid tribute to their temple goddesses. His mind has left its present life in pursuit of its new mission.

"Who's to say he's wrong? Who can say that changing reference frames will not make a positive difference in his life? His self immolation and the tearing up of his life no longer concern him. He knows that hellish consequences will surely come after he embraces and makes love to the irresistible flame that is Marty, but that no longer concerns him. He succumbs to his infatuation.

"He crosses an event horizon whereby his limbic zone mind merged with and controlled his cognitive mind. It is impossible to reverse course and turn back. After what he does next there will be no stopping the events that follow. He must make his vicarious dreams become reality. An unstoppable psychological force controls his behavior now. It is his certain belief that his dream world is possible. No force is more powerful. Nothing can oppose it. He picks up the phone. He calls Marty's Premium Member Service and makes an appointment to spend an hour with her. He has passed though a portal into a world that views morality differently from the way he viewed it before. He senses a terrible oppressive burden lifting away from him. He feels the fresh embrace of freedom."

George, nearly imperceptibly, nods to Marty. His feelings are exactly the same as his hypothetical man's. Before this day, like the man in his narration, it never would have occurred to George that new beliefs could replace his long-established ones. But it was happening. It was the consequence of Bertie's obsession. Her quest to forge his new life purpose opened George's eyes and mind to the acceptance of intimate artistry. Now, like his fictitious man, he too felt his old belief system give way. The new belief had long bubbled and percolated, like a magma chamber, beneath the surface of his feelings; charging, heating, and reheating, building up its explosive force until its chamber could no longer contain it. It needed to escape. Ultimately, like his fictitious viewer man, George's force expressed its powerful craving in a volcanic eruption.

George's love for Bertie was old landscape. It cracked and buckled as his underlying magma dome swelled and rose. Within the dome a shoot stream pushed upward through the belief body of George's emotional core; then it breached his surface composure and erupted. Its magnificent force was visible now. He made no effort to hide it from Bertie. It was an undeniably strong geyser, spurting skyward, showering its flows over George's old landscape, suffocating it. Like an ejaculation explosion from a penis, his new love order deified his newfound belief system. His eyes told Marty that he, like his fictitious viewing man, adored her and her film artistry; that he now venerated the glorious beauty of her immorality, as she expressed it so beautifully in her films and lifestyle. His eyes spoke truth to both his wife and the young sexpot. He loved her. Marty accepted George's nod with a knowing smile.

Bertie recognized the transitional nature of this moment. It was the foreseeable consequence of her newly discovered purpose. She needed Marty every bit as much or more than George needed Marty. Only by recruiting the young starlet to her cause of achieving notoriety could Bertie hope to put the tragedy of her daughter's death behind her. Bertie needed to close the door on her past life. Coaching her daughter and those endless hours of instruction and discipline that Olympic success required were finished. But, to close the door on that past life and move forward, Bertie knew she needed to close the door on her marriage to George as well, for George was a key part of her and her daughter's support system. Only by changing her relationship with George could Bertie finally close the door on the Olympic chapter of her life. She wasn't going to divorce George or throw him out of their home. She loved him far too much for that; but there needed to be an adjustment in their relationship.

Bertie needed to have time with Marty as both her coach and her lover; and to do that, Bertie needed George to discover a substitute love interest. Marty was the logical choice for that. Bertie understood that, by putting the two of them together in film work and in her family dynamic, nature would take its course. Her only concern was that Marty might reject advances from George, who was twenty-five years her senior. But thankfully, that was obviously not going to happen. Beyond Marty's proclivity to nymphomania, the young actress actually seemed attracted to George as a lover. George continued his narration:

"The wife sees and hears all of this. She imagines that the man on the silk sheets, his body caressed and nuzzled, his lips seductively kissed, and his penis lovingly stroked by Marty has become her husband. When Marty positions her partner's head upon a velvet pillow and removes her black bra and panties, the wife foresees that the same seductive reveal will befall her husband. The wife gasps while Marty kisses her partner's hands, places them upon her gorgeous breasts; then mounts his yearning shaft and commences her irresistible twerks and gyrations. The wife sees that Marty knows no modesty or shame; only immoral, sinful joy.

"*The film began with several men entering a church, carrying Marty upon their shoulders. Some men went before her to prepare her way. They swept away all the religious symbols from the altar and replaced its white cloth covering with a purple one, signifying the demise of innocence and the ascension of their new, immoral goddess. They arranged pillows upon the altar and lifted Marty upon it. She wore a loosely fitting purple gown which her assistants removed, revealing her nakedness. They then positioned her upon the pillows where she opened widely her legs. Her assistants then proceeded to kiss her mouth, fondle her breasts, and kiss her vagina.*

"*The priests of the church began shouting blasphemy. They tried to approach the altar to reclaim it; but they were restrained by Marty's retinue of believer-followers and turned back. They were further restrained and held captive behind a rope barrier which prevented them from interfering with the ceremony that was about to commence.*

"*Then a procession of worshippers, both men and women, began entering the church. They bore gifts of gold, jewels, and bundles of roses. One by one, these ardent believers in The New Morality Standard approached the altar and bowed to Marty. After they placed their gifts and roses at her feet, they approached her and kissed her hand, her mouth, or her vagina. She placed her hand upon each of their heads and told them that were now among those chosen to believe in the new moral order.*

"*The film had a thirty minute compilation section which showed five, six-minute vivid close-up scenes of Marty performing her most titillating explicit erotica. The wife gasped in disbelief while she watched Marty take penis head after penis head to her lips to lick and suck; and take testicle sac after testicle sac to her mouth where she licked and sucked them; and stroked penis shafts with her hands while she performed her exquisite fellatio, working her mouth in all sorts of ways upon the penises; taking them fully into her mouth and throat, bending them up and down with her teeth and jaw movements, stimulating them in ways the wife never had imagined possible.*

"And the wife witnessed Marty take the ejaculations of penis after penis onto her lips and onto her extended welcoming tongue. And she saw Marty smile and giggle and openly laugh at the successes of her partners' ejaculation's; congratulating them on their masculine prowess and on the prodigious amounts of semen they yielded up to her smiling, mirthful, mouth. What confounded the wife was that Marty seemed to know no shame or reticence over the salacious acts she was performing.

"The wife also saw penis after penis ejaculating into Marty's vagina. The cinematography vividly captured each penis as it shot its semen stream onto her opened vaginal lips or as it ejaculated while on the cusp of withdrawal from her vagina. Each compilation segment showed Marty's vagina oozing semen while she giggled and smiled and heaped effusive praise upon her sex partners for plying her so beautifully.

"Following the film's compilation segment, Marty commenced her fornication rituals. She sequentially hosted several lovers, mirthfully babbling and cooing her encouragement and praise to each; while simultaneously performing fellatio with other supplicants. Her partners, all, effusively praised her with professions of love, adoration, and wonder. After witnessing these Pagan fornication rites, three of the film's priests shed their raiment garb and knelt down, begging Marty's assistants for inclusion in the ceremony. These priests swore to disavow all belief in their former religion and pledged their undying fealty to the New Morality Standard. The were then permitted to approach the altar and fornicate with Marty. After they fornicated with her, she stood and hugged and kissed them; heaping praise upon them for their divinely inspired decision to convert to the New Morality Standard; and welcoming them to her newest Temple of Sins.

"The wife watching this film was stunned by what she was witnessing. At first, she could not comprehend the significance of the film. She could not fathom how any woman could perform fellatio and fornicate so openly and so freely with so many different sex partners and not feel the slightest shame or embarrassment or any scintilla of concern over her profligate, immodest whoring; nor could she fathom how so many different men and women could not only be unashamed to consort with such a profligate whore; but instead, how they could, in good conscience, heap adulations upon her for her licentiousness, and bestow honors upon her with and endless stream of money gifts, fine jewels, and celebratory roses. This shocking inversion of morality was incomprehensible to the spellbound wife.

"Her own life was so different. She was trained, from childhood, to be demure and modest. Her mother told her that she must be a good homemaker and mother; that she must never flaunt her desires; but when her husband wanted her to do her wifely duties, she needed to obey him. So, for this wife, sex was only something that her husband needed, not her; and it was her duty to comply with his needs. And if he sought pleasure elsewhere, that was perfectly understandable because men sometimes just did that. It was not her place to confront him about it or retaliate by seeking her own pleasures elsewhere. She was charged with finding her fulfillment in having her home provided for her. Beyond that, she needed to seek her comforts in the holy scriptures. Women she knew never made independent decisions. They obeyed their husbands. But here was this woman, this porn star, in this mind-altering film, doing such unimaginable things! What the wife was seeing seemed incomprehensible. How, she questions herself, her husband, and her marriage, could he choose to shower his wealth upon this wanton whore, when she, his dutiful wife, has cooked and cleaned for him all these years? Has she not given him sex whenever he wanted it?

"How, she ponders, has it become possible for men to give their unconditional love and boundless, adoring devotion to women who are profligate whores? Have men always been this way? Why, she wonders, is male lust so out in the open now? How could so many men bring themselves to serve up their very souls to a woman, such as our Marty, who revels unashamedly in her unremitting, licentious depravity? And how could they sustain their ardor with such fevered intensity, for a woman of flawed character like Marty? The wife intuitively knew she was observing a serious shift in social mores. This was not some transient fling between an errant husband and some hussie. She was seeing a bonding of souls; a rejection of old beliefs and a cementing of new beliefs; and a prideful honoring of the porn star's rejection of all moral teachings. Figuratively, Marty, in that film, represented humanity's rebirthing of the biblical golden calf. She was now the idol for these worshippers. She had become their God.

"What, the wife wondered, was she witnessing? She tried to place her mind into the minds of the people, especially the three priests, who capitulated their faith and were now honoring Marty. How could priests kneel on the very altar that they had used to worship for so many years; and now kneel before Marty on that same altar while performing cunnilingus with her? Then, suddenly, truth dawned upon the shaken wife.

"She had an epiphany. All became clear. The ceremony, the indoctrination of the priests, and Marty's role as Goddess, represented a changing in the world's moral ordering. A cultural shift was taking place. People were casting away their old God and their old religions, which had failed them and brought them to their terrible condition of world disorder. They were rejecting the religious, political, and legal orders which they had lived by for centuries, because they no longer believed in them. Instead, the people of the world were reposing their faith in Pagan prostitution worship. They would rather

trust the religious wisdom, political pronouncements, and legal decisions of their porn stars than leaders of their old-world order. People were turning over their power to the world's porn stars. How would these porn stars lead their followers; in what ways? Would the porn stars, the wife wondered, commit murders, like Bathsheba or Salome had? Would they turn their followers against traditional religionists; becoming tribal, like Pagans of millennia before? The wife shuddered. Fear and awe now displaced her wonderment.

"The people of the world were changing their Gods. They no longer wanted Gods that prescribed their behaviors and laid down laws to follow. They no longer wanted to obey the dictates of misogyny-based thinking. They wanted freedom and openness; and acceptance; and togetherness. They wanted to not blame or be blamed; not be faulted or find fault; not criticize or be criticized; not proscribe or be proscribed. Instead, they wanted to love and be loved; accept and be accepted; and to feel right and good about loving freely without inhibition or shame. Marty, the consummate purveyor of erotica, was the leader of this movement. In the film she assumed her natural, rightful role as its Goddess. These Pagan worshippers not only love Marty's pornographic films, they idolize her persona. They adore her and honor her. They worship and deify her. And they love her with all their hearts and souls and might. What incredible power and influence Marty has! Marty is their God!

"But where does this cultural change leave the wife? Before this day, the wife's world was perfectly ordered. She lived her life as her parents had told her to live it. She was a modest, moral woman who had married a good, stable husband with a promising future. She saved money in the bank and believed everything her government told her. Pornography was never something that could possibly concern her. Oh, she'd heard a radio promotion trailer about the new film we've worked on: 'LAY ROSES AT MY FEET.' In the brief clip she heard Marty chortle and coo about how much she loved making

the film; and how pleased she was with Bertie and George, her new performance coaches; and how the film was an instant box office sensation. The wife even saw a billboard with Marty's cherubic face and tantalizing lips saying: 'See my performance in LAY ROSES AT MY FEET.' But the radio clip and billboard were mere distractions for the serendipitous wife, until now.

"Synchronous thoughts now swiftly flowed between the wife's mind and her husband's. She feels his ardor towards her chill; his blood turn into frozen rivers of desensitized, compassionless ice; his heart turn to stone, as their dying romance freezes and shatters. But his same heart suddenly radiates with a new warmth. His excited blood courses hotly for our gorgeous Marty. The wife sees her husband's ardor for Marty swell and ripen. With his fateful phone call to Marty's Premium Service, the wife witnesses her husband's new-found love eruption, first hand.

"Our on-screen Marty chortles and smiles. She's ensconced among her velvet pillows in her maiden position, beaming confidently to the horrified wife through the camera lens. A partner rubs his penis head against Marty's warm, juicy, butterfly-winged peach, announcing its presence; then the penis begins to penetrate her silky, velvety- smooth, lubricated, glistening outer lips. Mortified, the wife understands that the man in the film will soon be her husband. She closes her eyes, momentarily hoping to block the naked truth from her world.

"Instead, her closed eyes see her husband's soul fly away from her; his back turned to her. He rushes, with open arms, toward his irretrievable destiny. Marty's soul smiles to him. She is proffering her shameless, iniquitous, 'there's nothing wrong with loving me,' smile. Her tongue moistens her lips. They quiver excitedly. She eagerly welcomes her newest convert to join her sinful revelry. The wife imagines her husband's and Marty's souls coming together. She watches their lips sharing a passionate kiss; then,

arm in arm, they fade away, departing the wife's imagination.

"The wife opens her eyes. She's numbed by her terror. Marty's semen filled vagina is shown, now magnified; taking up the entire screen. Marty's partner holds her vagina open to display her semen pool. Then her partner slowly pinches her vaginal lips closed. Remarkably, the semen in Marty's vagina rises to the outer lips of her vagina and rests there. The semen appears to be a living ball of white nectar being offered up upon the lips of a glorious pink rose; resembling an offering to lure a thirsting hummingbird.

"The camera slowly lifts. The wife's eyes follow. They pass by Marty's slowly undulating stomach, rising to her bountiful, heaving breasts and exhilarating, cherry-budded nipples, settling upon our darling's prideful, beaming face. The camera keeps the wife's eyes fixated to the screen. It slow-frames every motion of Marty's mouth. Marty's fingers casually retrieve semen from her vagina and bring it to her lips. The wife gasps! She's mortified. She's never imagined a woman could so proudly flaunt her shameless wantonness. Seductively, shamelessly, Marty passes her tongue over her lips. She presses her tongue against the lower teeth of her opened mouth; and casually receives the semen offering into her immoral mouth. The wife interprets this scene as the spilling of seed. It is the consignment of life's purposeful goodness to eternal evil. She believes Marty's pornography mocks God's creation commandment. It explicitly portrays human defilement of conception; substitutes pleasure for procreation as the real purpose for human copulation.

"Marty's partner now reclines by her side. He is not finished expressing his love for her. Marty casually rolls her head to her left to discover another penis positioned next to her lips. She begins performing fellatio on the penis. Meanwhile the wife's imaginary husband, stimulates her clitoris and prepares her vagina to receive yet a third penis. The imaginary husband kisses Marty's right nipple. And when she rolls her head back to the right, he kisses her

mouth. He has not only spilled his seed into Marty; he is also signifying that he has also surrendered his soul to her; that he fully endorses all that she does; all the immorality that she represents; and that he will do everything he can humanly do to pleasure her and facilitate her whoring., including the surrendering of his family's assets to her."

"Does my description adequately describe that scene, Marty?" George looked at the nymph and smiled his knowing smile to her.

"*Yes, George. It does,*" she beamed.

"*And were you enjoying the creation of that scene?*"

"*Yes, George; very much.*"

"*And you had no problem with having sex with another partner while semen from your first partner was still in your vagina?*"

"*Ha, George! You're so provincial! Of course not. Semen is a wonderful lubricant. I love doing my partners in sequence. It heightens my mood and makes me even more eager to make love than before.*"

"*And your partners have no issues with that?*"

"*Goodness no, George! When a man's penis head slides against my lady lips that penis receives the hottest, juiciest, slipperiest sensations it has ever known. The man who is entering me has a limbic flood that drowns out all other feelings and thoughts. He's experiencing nirvana. He instantaneously becomes addicted to having sex with me. There's no room in his mind for anything or anyone else.*"

"*Not even his wife?*"

"*Especially not his wife, George. His wife becomes a thing of the past.*"

"*Instantly?*"

"*Instantly.*"

"*Promise?*"

"*Promise.*"

"I see. And while you were performing that explicit scene, did it occur to you that somewhere out there in the world of viewers there might be someone's wife who became mortified, knowing that you are perfectly capable of stealing her husband away from her?"

"Well, that happens, George. It simply happens, that's all," smiled Marty, innocently.

"And that doesn't affect your conscience? I mean, you don't fee guilty about hurting another woman?"

"No, George, not at all. I never allow those thoughts to enter my mind. I only allow myself to think about my pleasure and the copulating I'm performing in that scene."

Marty again smiled, shrugging her shoulders, indicating that the pornography business was simply about creating glorious explicit erotica; and not about providing emotional support to those it adversely affected.

"Tell us, you sweet, innocent nymph, what got you into doing porn in the first place?"

"Well, George, I had already come to think of myself as a very promiscuous girl. I was already doing my classmates' boyfriends. And I loved wearing provocative outfits that showed off my boobs and my tush. I get lots of compliments about my boobs and my tush, you know. And, I honestly love the freedom of being naked; and I love fucking, more than doing anything else in the world. So, when the opportunity came for me to have sex as a career choice; and also get well paid for having sex, I felt like I couldn't resist the opportunity. And once I started creating porn, I discovered I loved creating it. It opened up so many opportunities; and they all involved having even more sex. So, here we are!"

"And you never feel any guilt about doing one man right after another; no concern for your partners' feelings or jealousy feelings from other women?"

"Absolutely none, George. As I told you, I absolutely love to fuck. I have no morals; none. Don't try to overthink my character, George. I'm a whore to my core; fuck bunny; slut; and I love my life; and I feel no shame in it because there is no shame in it. My shrink, Mrs. O'Dell, assures me that pornography simply represents the honest reversion to humanity's natural worship practices; to how people worshipped before five or six thousand years ago; before the power crazed misogynists hijacked tribal worship practices and perverted them into confining religions."

"There you have the essence of the Marty phenomenon, Bertie." George turned toward his wife with his eyebrows raised, indicating his enlightenment. *"The world's morality is a mortally wounded ship. It carries all of society on board, and it is doomed to sink into the depths of a deep ocean's abysmal abyss. There, social fabric is shredded by the dark creatures who dwell there, until all the norms we now know dissolve and disintegrate. There, in the cold, dark abyss, humanity searches for a new guidance compass to be its God and to lead it. Society is sliding into the depths of its abyss now, Bertie. Society's new leadership God is opening her arms to receive new believers and welcome them to the abyss. This new God is becoming more and more visible. And the new God is Marty, the most profligate and incorrigible of all porn stars who populate the abyss. She is the beacon light of humanity's new future, don't you see, Bertie? She will take humanity's soul and resurrect it from the dark abyss. The more we cast her films as the antagonist to traditional religion and morality, the more her star will rise. She will be deified. A new order will arise from our miserable abyss of dishonesty and corruption; and Marty will lead the new order. Do you see that, Bertie? Do you see that, Marty?"*

"Yes, George, I see it," smiled Bertie. She was happy to adopt the new perspective. She had already become disillusioned with God because He took her Amanda from her.

"So, you want me to perform in a new film these scenes which attack the religious and social order? Is that right?" Marty's curiosity was piqued. She visualized the potentials for fame and stardom by associating herself with Bertie and George's new film themes.

"Yes, you gorgeous femme!" George lifted his arms in exaltation. His effusive sales enthusiasm had erupted. Obviously, he saw the enormous financial potential for films that advocated a new religious concept. *"You will be cast in ways that mock God and the ordered fabric of society. Would you be okay with that?"*

"Will my porn star ratings go up?" Marty, in her heart of hearts, was a true mercenary.

"Trust me," George smiled confidently, *"They will skyrocket! We are simply identifying a trend and placing you in front of it. You will lead it and expand it by adding millions of followers. The world will salivate for more and more of you."*

"I'll be happy to perform in your new film themes, George, and Bertie. I'll be forever grateful to both of you."

"Then, you'll have no qualms about playing roles that pit you as the antagonist to religion and the social order?"

"No problem, George. Those already are my honest feelings. I have no problem living my life that way. I'm happy with who I am and with everything I do. Okay? Of course, I'll perform. I'll give you one hundred percent plus effort!"

"Okay, good. Just checking. Well, back to the film study. Assume this scene you were performing terrorized our fictional wife. She feared you were tearing her husband, her whole life, away from her. And, she's right. You were tearing some husbands away from their wives with that film, weren't you, Marty?"

"Well, I certainly hope so. I'd like to think my sex appeal trumps most other women's." An innocent, confident smile passed Marty's lips.

"Oh, trust me, sweetheart, it does. But, Bertie, here's where I think our films can cause some foreseeable and tragic consequences. Our delicious darling is now smiling her innocent sexuality to the wife through the camera lens; but the wife intuits that the smile communicates a beguiling taunt. She cringes before Marty's iniquitous message. She interprets the luster sheen in Marty's eyes as the demonic gleam of an evil she-devil. I mean, her mind is coming from the time when women, like Marty, were perceived to be witches.

"The wife stares, mesmerized, fantasizing; imagining an ominous stream of poisoned darts shooting out from Marty's eyes, piercing her God-abiding heart. She feels her life, and everything she stands for and believes in, is falling victim to our sexpot harlot's murderous toxins. She recognizes Marty's beguiling, pleasured smile, for what it is. She thinks those confident, sinful, devil lips have targeted her and are now messaging her. She sees Marty's pursing kisses and smile as a dismissive, kiss-off smile from her godless conqueror.

"The wife's mind races. She imagines that our sex goddess had communicated specifically to her, through her film, and that the battle for her husband's affections is already over. The wife correctly intuits that unmerciful Marty has won this contest, before even meeting her husband. She further imagines, panicked, that her husband's soul is falling, like a helpless victim fly slips from the lip of a silken, slippery pitcher plant, into Marty's soul-drowning well. Downward, irresistibly falling, the wife sees her husband's soul slide helplessly into the abysmal sweetness of Marty's sinful soul-pit. The wife knows that, once her husband's soul falls into Marty's pit, the minx will surely, remorselessly dissolve all the goodness his soul ever had; absorbing it into her immoral essence; further strengthening her immoral, iniquitous powers.

"The wife's spirits plunge. Her heart sinks. Until this past half-hour she didn't comprehend that a battle for her husband's soul *was raging inside his mind. She fleetingly hoped reality and reason would return and repossess her husband. But that hope shattered when he placed the call to Marty's Premium Service. The wife's entire body is now swept with a foreboding chill. She senses her feelings are trapped; held captive under icy cold water. She can't escape the numbing coldness. Horror of horrors, her husband is leaving her! For a heartless, immoral adult film actress! Horrors!*

"The wife knows her husband's path will surely deliver him into Marty's clutches. Belatedly, she realizes that pornography is not some abstract concept that exists in some imaginary world a million miles away from her. It's here, in her home. It's real! It's her reality; her nightmare. She's witnessing it, face to face; in the present. It is being viewed. No, not being viewed; being casually studied and obsessed and drooled over; by her beloved husband, no less. Our beguiling porn star has captivated her husband's heart; seized it from her. Obviously, he vicariously LOVES Marty! The wife clearly sees Marty threatens her ordered world.

"She is especially terrified that her husband obsesses over one particular porn star. She can't hide her indignity behind the generalized façade that her husband became addicted to porn. That's not what's happened. He's become smitten by Marty's beguiling eyes and her trademarked butterfly foo-foo. Kudos to Bertie's marketing genius! Marty has captured this husband's soul. She can do as she wishes with him: love him; play him for a fool; use him, take his money; even murder him and dispose of him if she chooses. He's completely within her power and he has not even met her or made love with her; not yet.

"Fear tightens its grip on the wife's heart. Her husband is not seeing Marty as an amusement or distraction. He's getting something much more profound from her 'ROSES' film. He's receiving love from it. It's more than whimsical fantasy love. This love binds souls;

like fast drying glue. It doesn't wash off. It cements her husband to Marty, permanently. It gives him an eros feeling that he must have and which the wife cannot give.

"Worse! he seeks to convert Marty's film images to real flesh on flesh contact; experience actual physical lovemaking with her; glue his body to hers, as well as his mind and soul. The wife sees he's mesmerized by Marty's seductress performance in this particular film. She knows his moral learning's fell, like shredded corpses on a battlefield. Those learned do's and don'ts were always abstract concepts. They never faced a determined enemy like Marty, before. Their indoctrinated taboo pronouncements were hopelessly overmatched. Marty decimated them like they were light infantry, charging artillery at point blank range. His religious belief averments also fell and died, impaled by Marty's sword. They lost to his own unstoppable limbic eruptions, caused by our captivating, iniquitous, glorious darling. His limbic mind raced across his imaginary battlefield, stepping over the dead bodies of morality and religion; rushing onward, furiously, blindly, with open arms to his new savior, Marty, and her glorious cornucopia of boundless sinful pleasures." George gave Marty a loving hug; then he continued:

"What caused this tragedy, the wife wonders? She lifts her eyes to the screen again. She focuses on the slow-motion frame sequence. Bertie's genius rivets the wife's attention to the full screen display. It purposely lingers on Marty's sex. The wife is confronted by Marty's provocative film scene. There it is! In the wife's face! It's gorgeous, breathtaking! It's like a ripened, juicy peach offering sustenance to a desert wanderer. It's not just any vagina. It has butterfly wings! It's trademarked. It only belongs to Marty. It loves copulating so much that it figuratively purrs pleased feline purrs from the screen to its viewers. Marty's beckoning vagina silently informs the wife that it

is the opposite of everything the wife represents. It has become her husband's life goal and salvation. It's a mock and husband-refuge sanctuary from the wife's social gatherings, parties, neighborly visits, PTA meetings, church services, stresses, pretenses, and obligations.

"It's a male's escape from all the ties that bind husbands to wives. The wife feels her chill grow colder. She now knows her husband desperately needs the relief promised by our darling nymph. His attraction to her honest, straightforward offering is real. Buried beneath the harsh demands of his married life, there had always lurked a dormant craving for just such a sanctuary. It time-bubbled, building pressure and volume. It became angry volcanic magma. Marty's honest immorality succeeded. It weakened the wife's ties to her husband; melted away the layers of guilt that previously held him in place; uncorked his frustrations; permitted him to release his magma; explode away all obstacles to attaining Marty's seductive passions.

"This is frightfully different from the husband's occasional flirts and indiscrete straying eyes. The wife always coped with those annoyances. But now she finds herself facing a frontal onslaught against morality itself. Our incorrigible intimacy actress is mercilessly crushing the wife's way of life under the treads of an unstoppable, relentlessly immoral, unapologetic, take no prisoners, battle tank. Marty is crushing and grinding the wife's moral ways into dust; murdering her pathetic righteous forces like they are helplessly overmatched infantry.

"The wife doesn't know her enemy. She thinks it's Marty; but it's not Marty. It dwells within her husband. It's his need. His wife offers him yakablabery, pretenikery, mindnumery; all served up in heaping spoonfuls of meaningless contorted, illogically convoluted blather-spewed righteous stew. He MUST escape it; else his spirit will die; his maleness will expire.

"Marty represents honest, straightforward simplicity in a recognizable, simple format. She understands his need; and she willingly, freely offers it. She offers love, of a sort; not the tied-down, placed in a domestic harness version of love. It's the instant gratification kind of love; the lust assuaging kind; but it is, nevertheless, a form of understanding, loving, love. It is the passion union of two souls that deeply crave each other's intimacy.

"Their souls seek escape into passion. It's born of pheromones' attractions. There's no deep thinking involved in this primal, pagan form of lust-love. There's no meeting of common interests, hobbies, or cultures, or experiences; no wine and dine dates with chocolates and baubles; none of those sorts of things. It's pure unadulterated lust for flesh touchings and sex. It's the deeply honest, physical human love that the husband needs. It's the deeply seated urge-need to fuck. It's his reincarnated, modern-day cave man; grab woman by her hair; drag her to cave; ravage her body; dominate her; pump semen into her; raw lovemaking kind of love. It's demonstrably explicit, erotic, romantic, animal attraction-animal gratification love. It's Marty's love specialty.

"Our darling nymph goddess brooks no quarter. Marty plays for keeps in her film role, effortlessly conquering lover after lover; penis after penis. She is brazened, remorseless, unapologetic, and shameless. She sits upon her pillowed throne, surrounded by eager, stiffened cocks. She fondles the balls of the man in front of her and takes his penis into her mouth; first licking it enthusiastically from scrotum to tip. Obvious to the horrified wife, Marty loves what she's doing. She honestly declares so:

'I LOVE YOUR PENIS. I COULD SUCK YOUR PENIS ALL DAY LONG,' she coos articulately and lovingly.

"The husband watching this knows that Marty means every word. He can't resist Marty for another second. He must have her. The premium service takes the husband's call. The wife, in the *deepest pit of her gut, knows that our real-life nymph goddess will be as salaciously immoral and conscience-free as the roles she plays in her films. She shudders. She is as fearful as the hapless mortals who faced deadly combat with unconquerable Achilles. She knows our glorious Queen of Wantonness and her trademarked profligate vagina will not hesitate to impale her with her heartless lust-spear; steal her husband from her. Marty will show her no mercy. She fully understands that Marty will impale her marriage with her lust-spear; remorselessly murdering it.*

"The wife becomes frenzied. She trembles, knowing Marty's threat to her world is real. She had hints that this day was coming. Everything she believed in was getting turned upside down and inside out. The banks were becoming unstable. Her friends were buying gold, silver, and farmland. Her government fiat money purchased less and less. She watched morality's decline for years. She observed accelerating social decay. Pleasantries were scarcer. Friendships were fractured into opposing political camps. Thieves, muggers, and beggars now controlled her city's streets. Children learned ridiculous attitude posturing in school; not reading, writing and arithmetic. The teacher union teachers no longer taught. The kids knew their teachers no longer cared about them; that they were only out for themselves. Boys became violent animals. Girls became promiscuous tarts. People fornicated openly in public places and theaters. Inner cities were overrun by anarchists. The former President's averred goal of fundamentally transforming America was happening. The Shining City on the Hill was becoming a cesspool for degenerates; a mirror image of the former President's own mind. The wife had stopped going downtown years ago. People trapped in urban rot pleaded for help. But help did not come. The inner cities couldn't be saved.

"Social decay had never bothered the wife before. But now she saw anarchy in her suburb too. 'What is happening to my country?'

she wonders. She looks to the First lady; but alas! The President's wife spews hatred for America, dresses in anarchists' black and red, and does nothing to moderate her husband's ill intentions. Our wife turns to her church. Alas again! Her church was closed down by the government. A priest had prophesied earlier that freedom of religion in America was dying. That hadn't concerned her, until now. But now, everything suddenly seemed more bothersome.

"She feels a stealthy chaos creeping up on her. Lawlessness seems closer to her doorstep than before. Her friends openly defy what the government tells them about some horrible disease. They ignore precautions, willfully disregard government guidelines. They laugh at government edicts; scorn them. They've stopped trusting government's leaders. She doesn't know whom to trust or what to think. The government's people, who are supposed to know these things, seem more ignorant than she. They give conflicting pronouncements, disobey their own guidelines, making it hard to vest them with credibility. Government pronouncements about acceptable forms of thought expression perplex her. Pornography is championed by government as the new national religion. The Government attacks traditional religious institutions; orders that her church limit congregation sizes and occasionally orders her church to close down.

"Some friends secretly go to invitation-only sex partnering parties and clandestine orgy meetings. Others stopped wearing safety masks and resumed attending secret church services. She assumed those asocial behaviors could not affect her life. But everything is topsey turvey.

"Social fabric has badly frayed. Friends expect her to believe that immorality and prostitution are acceptable. She's told there's a New Modern Morality Standard that glorifies prostitution; but her old morality is ingrained in her. Her old ways are more comfortable. The world is changing fast, but she is unable to change with it. She

feels alone, trying desperately to climb an imposing wall of uncaring, immoral ice. She only slips further down this rigid uncompromising wall. She's failing badly. Her confusion gives way to fear. It sweeps over her like an untamed flood from a dam break. The prospect of imminently drowning in an immoral sea terrifies her.

"This wife misjudged a profound change. Marty, the star of our film, is adulated and honored for her wanton debauchery! Her film partners message that she is their divine goddess. They praise her gloriously pure immorality. They and her legions of fans categorize Marty's performances as the ultimate in Avant Garde erotic romantic artistry. They do not consider Marty's artistic expressions of explicit eroticism to be pornographic; not really: not in the old sense.

"Rather, modern day film critics regard her film scenes as breathtakingly beautiful; indelibly glorious, savory morsels of film artistry; rich in their passionate expressiveness; a triumph of feelings' shameless honesty. One reviewer calls her work 'genius' for the way she effortlessly conveys the feelings she's experiencing in her copulation scenes. Another review columnist says: 'You cannot watch Marty's films and not fall in love with her;' and another: 'Her emotional honesty will warm your heart and cling to your soul.'

"The wife's idea of romance was always different. A handsome prince on a white horse was supposed to come. He was supposed to sweep her, the innocent maiden, off her feet and whisk her away to his magic kingdom. Maybe the hero and heroine were supposed to fight, then make up, kiss, and fall in love, like the well-trodden plot path in so many formulaic romance novels. Maybe the prince finally got to have his way with her. So be it. She would smile while she felt the heat of his thrusts. Good for both of them! Those romances were so much safer and more mentally manageable. There were no triggers to upset the wife. Well, perhaps a few little triggers; but those

came with plenty of warnings. The wife's psyche could cope with them. Those were acceptable eroticism.

"But not this! No, never this! Not this film's lewd, wanton portrayal of a world where a woman heroine lusts after sex and lovers in such a welcoming, uninhibited shameless way. The wife is aghast! Marty's debauchery, and the ways she flaunts it are incomprehensible! They tear away the veil of feminine modesty. Never before this, could the wife imagine hearing another woman saying things like: 'I can't believe I'm so lucky that all you men want to fuck me!' And: 'I love how your semen tastes!' And 'This is so much fun!' And 'I love the way you are all so sweet with me!'

"And all the while Marty is saying these encouraging things to her partners, she is laughing and giggling; rollicking carefree and casual in her immoral glee. Never before this could the wife imagine any woman so enthralled with fornication; so eager to reciprocate the thrusts of her male partners; so shamelessly obsessed with sating her own libido. It's far too much for the wife to process! Too shocking! It assaults all bounds of the wife's propriety! She is shaken beyond mere discomfort. She trembles. Her legs feel weak beneath her. The overwhelming force of Marty's sexuality slams her consciousness. Her sensibilities are rocked to her core.

"It's a furious typhoon confronting an unsuspecting vessel. Marty's audaciously unrepentant vagina, flowing its greedy rivulets of vanquished semen, is the storm's eye of the wife's sudden turmoil. From nowhere, from the calm blankness of her peaceful home with the television screen usually its blank, black, turned off position, this pornography, this whirlwind that will upend her life, appeared. Her marriage and life are captured, unprepared, in the storm's furious swells and winds, now passing directly over her husband and lifting him aloft into its insatiable need for more fuel to feed it; sucking his life away from her; leaving her with nothing.

"*This Marty, this ravenous porn star, is a taker. She takes what she wants; now targets her precious husband to annihilate his morals. This film and its Marty heroine deify carnal immorality. Yet, the horrified wife acknowledges, the film was done beautifully and tastefully. Starlet Marty and her lovers performed their explicit eroticism romantically and sincerely. The wife is aghast; feeling stunned, shocked; helpless.*

"*The choreography and the shockingly upsized fornicating genitalia scenes glorify Marty's seduction prowess, making her lady lips appear bigger than life itself. The film's artistry spellbinds. The husband's limbic mind is sucked into the whirlwind of Marty's insatiable butterfly winged vagina. He shocks the wife when she hears him place his call to Marty's service. His capitulation contrasts sharply with the wife's preconceived ideas of pornography. She is dazed. She stares again at the screen. This time she focuses on Marty's face. It's a beautiful, sweetly-innocent looking face; the kind of face sons seek to marry. The wife tries to create order out of her disordered world.*

"*She visualizes Marty as an innocent virgin bride, bedecked in a traditional white wedding dress, preceded by cherub girls tossing rose pedals; being walked demurely down a church aisle by her proud father, about to be given to a handsome, appreciative groom; a sacred, unblemished, precious virgin gift, delivered into the holy sacrament of marriage. Nostalgic tears come to the wife's eyes, reminding her of her own more innocent times. She imagines hearing Wagner's anticipatory 'Here Comes the Bride." and the triumphant refrains from Mendelssohn's 'Wedding March.' Those were fitting bookends at her own wedding, solemnifying the sacred union of man and woman before family, friends, and almighty God.*

"*The wife's nostalgia dissipates; replaced by numbing shock. Marty is not religious. She does not seek traditional marriage. If anything, she's blasphemous. No, blasphemy is merely profaning God's name. Marty represents something far worse. She lashes out at God; challenges God's very existence; invades minds of innocents, like the wife's husband, and tears their souls away from God by presenting her ravaging vagina, in flagrante delicto; as a far better alternative to God. Marty is openly engaging in pitched battle with God for the moral souls of men.*

"Prostitutes, like Marty, were once tolerated, as long as they kept to their affairs in dark, quiet places. No longer! Now, as porn stars, these celebrated women proudly mock and defile Godliness before the entire world. They brazenly challenge social order. And, by their many viewing fans, they are loved for doing it. The wife now realizes there is a new world order arising from today's social dystopia; a world she heretofore could not imagine."

GEORGE'S SURRENDER

No terms, except your unconditional and immediate surrender, can be accepted. (General Ulysses S. Grant to the commander of Confederate Forces at the battle of Fort Donelson, controlling Tennessee's Cumberland River)

Marty moved her face closer to George's and smiled innocently and warmly. It was not a subtle smile. It was more like the successful smile of a knowing cat that had just eaten a defenseless canary. She blinked her eyes at George, holding her lashes closed for a longer than normal seductive moment.

"Do you really believe my eyes have the demonic gleam of a she-devil, George? Do you like the ways I defile God? Do you think I'm good at it? Will you help me get even better at it?" Marty smiled, giving a coquettish turn of her head while mouthing a kiss to

George. She rubbed her index finger slowly, seductively across her lower lip; then, with a second, partial, come-hither turn of her head, she followed her finger motion exactly; this time with her tongue, inviting George to join his lips to hers. Her signals were unmistakable.

"To our imaginary wife, yes; to me, no. I think you have warm, loving eyes. And, yes, I will help you become better at defiling God. I'm honored to assist you." George smiled to his nympho love interest. His voice reassured Marty that he was serious.

"And, George, do you feel that perhaps your own soul is like that hapless fly, sliding helplessly into my immoral abyss?" Marty pressed her body next to George's. Softly, her hand squeezed and tugged his cock.

"Honestly, yes. My demise seems unavoidable. I feel myself sliding, falling." George's eyes confessed his building passion.

"Is my immorality really striking you like a furious typhoon, George? Are you really feeling like a helpless vessel which is about to capsize into my sea of bottomless sins?"

"Unfortunately; no, fortunately, yes. I am floundering, about to capsize. I cannot resist you. I'm about to drown in your irresistible wantonness."

"Do you honestly believe sinning with me would be such a bad thing, George? Would you rather fly away from me and escape?" Another eye blink and smile followed Marty's question.

"No, I think not. I suppose I want to continue falling. I want you to swallow me up. I don't want to resist what I know will be wonderful. Bertie wants this for me; for all of us. I appreciate her goal. But I believe I need to discover for myself what it feels like to be immersed in your immoral abyss. Intimacy is, after all, a personal matter." George's hapless melancholy smiles signaled Marty that he had the soul of an innocent, trusting child.

"It is, George. And I respect that. And you know I have intimacy with my film partners, Premium Members, and lovers. Do you wish to join them, and dissolve your soul in my immoral sin pit? You can't be jealous of any of them, George. I forbid jealousy. You can never blame me or try to make me feel guilty for leading you astray. Do you understand? Once you involve your life with mine, you may never have your soul back. You'll be immersed in my private abyss. You'll be inside my nymphomania with me. I can't help myself, George. I can't change and I don't want to. Promiscuity fulfills me. It's who I am." Marty's eyes questioned the older George, as if to suggest he had no idea what torment he was wishing upon himself.

"Yes, I understand completely, But I feel I must. I'm not afraid; I have no thoughts of ever escaping you." George shook his head slowly, his wan smile communicating to Marty he would accept his future, come whatever may come. If he was anything, George was honest.

"I love you, George. You're a very sweet man. I love you and I want to give you pleasures. I want you to know that." Marty's kiss was the softest, most seductively honest kiss that George's lips had ever felt. The anxious would-be lovers understood they needed to wait for their moment. George's anxious heart beat faster. He continued:

"There's a profound shift in societal norms taking place. It has blindsided this hapless, unsuspecting wife. She wonders how this could have happened. And how could it have happened so quickly? How could everything she believes in get challenged and ripped away from her by some chortling, giggling, shameless whore in some porn film? In the film's trailer, Marty proudly proclaimed that film proceeds will be contributed to the New Modern Morality Standard. The trailer revealed that Marty's foundation will groom young women who seek careers in prostitution. Hearing about this frontal assault on morality, the wife feels knocked on her head. This new

reality should not be true! It's inconceivable! This brazen Marty, this sex star, openly advocates that prostitution is a desirable career choice for young women! The wife thinks someone must stop this heathen woman; censor her; and declare her films illegal. She thinks:

'To hell with the Constitution's First Amendment! Her films are destroying our culture and ruining our country!'

"She wonders whether her own precious daughters might succumb to the brazen allure of promiscuous whoredom. Her paranoia causes her so much angst that she begins pulling out her hair. Next, a foreboding image flashes through her frenzied mind. Her clueless, mullet, husband-dunce leaves his secure depths to bask-flop foolishly on the ocean's surface. Soulless Harpy Marty perched on an overhanging branch, sees her fool meal-fish husband signal-flash his defenseless belly. Our glorious raptor whore, opportunistic fish-hawk that she is, swoops.

"Alarm! Horrors! The wife intuits that hapless mullet husbands are staple diet fare for Marty. Too late! Marty's razor-sharp talon hooks have already sunken into her husband's flesh. Our glorious divine raptor-eagle easily lifts the woman's mullet husband away from his wife's world. Her irresistible vagina acts as a fatal hallux talon. He is captured and bound by it. She methodically devours his soul at her leisure. Secure; alone in her feasting nest, Marty seductively devours her husband's soul; dissolves it into her own. He becomes a disciple follower; worshipping her immoral ways.

"Panicked by her own imagery, the wife becomes horrified at the thought of losing her husband. With one fateful phone call he has left her world. She can't comprehend his betrayal. Her entire adult life, she did everything a good wife is expected to do. She slaved like a dutiful dog to keep their marriage intact and their household solvent. She indulged his whims, even his moronic addiction to that abhorrent, mindless, idiotic game of football; and now she realizes their money is going to disappear into the ravenous vagina and sex

craven mouth of a shameless, iniquitous woman of leisure, whose plies her explicit erotica as pleasure sport; against whom she is inadequate to compete with, sexually. She knows any effort to rekindle romance with her husband would be foolhardy; doomed from the start.

"The wife assesses herself. She's skinny, timid, and miserable. She approaches life like a frightened rabbit; fearful of falling into poverty; scared of being shunned by family, friends, and church. Experimenting in extramarital adventures terrifies her. She closes her mind to new ideas and new experiences. She even forbids herself the company of other men as friends.

"Marty is her diametric and diabolical opposite. She's beautiful, well endowed with physical attributes every woman wishes she had. Her breasts are voluptuous and young. Unlike the wife's pendulant bags, Marty's breasts up-lilt, her areolas serving up pink-red bud nipples like tasty, succulent cherries which beg to be kissed and suckled. And Marty is shamelessly profligate! How can a woman so beautiful and with such well-endowed anatomy revel in sinfulness instead of thanking and serving God for her bounty, as some man's good wife? How can she be so evil, the wife ponders? She can not understand Marty. Her mind can not process that another woman could believe cavorting with so many men is good and glorious. The wife can not comprehend that immorality and sin are irrelevant, alien concepts to our darling Marty."

Marty, hearing George refer to her by the endearing term 'darling,' slow blinked her eyes and smiled her warm appreciation to George. Her face told him that her sex was moist and eager to make love with him. Her finger touches firmed while she continued stroking his penis.

"George, tell me what you think." Marty pursed her lips in a mock innocent pout. *"Do you honestly think my promiscuity is sinful?"* Her fingers squeezed his penis with slightly more pressure.

She pushed down against it while making her strokes more rapid. *"Does my promiscuity offend you, or does it arouse you? Do you think my love making is boring or evil; or do you think it's beautiful and healthy?"*

George took a deep breath. He was close to ejaculation. He imagined their love making was already happening. He marveled at the emotive empathy streaming from Marty's eyes. He willed himself to focus. Obviously, the vixen sought his approving complements. Her confident smile conveyed her promise of intimacy, while her fingers tapped and stroked his penis, affirming her sincerity.

"No, Marty, it is glorious and beautiful, never evil. But does it really matter what I think?" George returned her smile with a wan smile of his own. He breathed deeply, savoring her scent wafts. His mouth salivated. His modest head shake was his playful signal telling her he was anxious to capitulate. He looked forward to becoming Marty's newest conquest. He was only waiting for Bertie's film sequence reviews to end. Then, he would happily surrender to her. He imagined unimaginable pleasures while she devoured his soul.

"Oh, yes George," Marty's cooing tone had a sinfully delicious, teasing quality. *"I could not stand myself if you thought I was dull or evil. I don't believe I could live with that. I just could not bear the thought of that."*

"No, you are not dull or evil, Marty." George's reassurance was intended to bolster her ego and, hopefully, raise her libido to even greater heights. He imagined a time in the near future when he would press Marty's naked body close to his, kiss her passionately; touch her vagina, open her; and make love with her. He wrestled with his impulse feeling. It would not be the coming together of two love starved souls; it wouldn't be anything enduring. No, not for either of them. It would be transient; perhaps nothing really special for her, given her porn profession and her many lovers;

yet, it was a moment he would die for. He ached for their 'when' moment. He knew he would love and savor it.

And he knew beforehand that he would fall hopelessly in love with her; accept all her immoral ways; her other lovers. Perhaps it was how her mind worked? Perhaps it was her casual innocence about all of it? He could not reason the why of it; but he knew he wanted her; all of her. Her face and lips, her body; and her mind: and her ways of thinking about life. All of her. He gathered his thoughts. He needed to elaborate his response:

"You, yourself, do not believe your performances are boring or evil. And I do not think of you in any way other than as a creative artisan; and your performances are beautiful, spellbinding. And you are a playful and naughty genius with your eroticism, and the splendid ways you present it. You captivate. There are righteous types who think all erotic actresses are evil; but you'll never see me thinking that way. You could make another thousand explicit films, Marty; and neither I, nor your millions of followers, would ever think any one of your film scenes were boring, or evil. I've always thought of you and your work as evocative and stimulating; breathtaking, actually. I don't believe I'll ever be able to get enough of you or your work."

"I've also heard you mention glorious." Marty fished for more compliments. She loved George's feedback. *"Is that how you honestly feel about me when you watch me making love?"*

"Yes, Marty, ravishing and glorious. You transport my libido to other worlds." George responded sincerely. He could tell Marty valued his opinion. *"Honestly, your love making is glorious. You are the living definition of glorious. Your expressions when you orgasm are the most glorious expressions that I've ever witnessed from any screen actress in all my life. You uniquely express the pure wonderment and beauty of intimacy like no other actress ever could. Everything about you, and all that you do, is beautiful and glorious. Of course, it is. You are a darling, Marty."*

"Oh George, you are so sweeeeet!" Marty's relief was genuine. In moments like this her emotions could effervesce, like those of an innocent child receiving approval from her schoolmaster. *"Thank you. I had to ask. I had to know how you felt about me. It's important to me."* Marty leaned into George and kissed his cheek.

Marty's kiss strengthened his vitality. His hardness confirmed his appreciation. His penis visibly strained against his pants. But for Bertie's watchful presence, George would already be undressing Marty. He continued his imaginary scenario about the infatuated husband and his distraught wife:

"Our darling Marty approaches life unafraid and confident. Whatever she wants, she assumes she will have. Erotic romantic involvements are her smorgasbord. She partakes and casually enjoys as she pleases. This is perfectly natural for her. Lovers are there for her pleasure to explore, seduce and devour, like low hanging fruits in an orchard of bountiful trees. This confidence in life's loves shows in her films. Life is good to Marty. It loves her, as she loves it."

THE GLORIOUS PEACH

All the privilege I claim for my own sex...... (Jane Austen: Persuasion)

"Ultimately, our distraught wife's eyes fixate on Marty's sex. Illumined by Bertie's alternating pink-and-orange-colored light filters, it's presented as a luscious, pulsating juicy peach; polished-waxed to lustrous, buttery soft smoothness. The light magic accents her beautifully translucent butterfly wings. The effect enchants. Her alluring peach beckons her partners, welcoming penis after penis to enter the lubricated, silky-smooth channel. Its wings flutter romantically, lovingly, with each visiting penis. It cavorts erotically, imparting genuine passion to each visitor. Penis after penis thrusts in copulation bliss, meeting the responding flutters of the iniquitous, playful

peach. Peach Butterfly and penis dance mystically, rhythmically, beautifully.

"While witnessing Marty's glorious, spellbinding spectacle, the wife gasps. Marty's sex resembles a procession of carefree butterflies enthralled in glorious mating dances above Mexico's jungle canopy. Each partner penis becomes mindlessly absorbed in its pleasure dance; then ejaculates wildly into the butterfly peach's warm, silky eternity.

"The camera again focuses an extreme close up on Marty's delicious peach, displayed full screen between her widespread butterfly wings. Her sex's waxen smoothness beckons viewers to sample her delightful, juicy flavors. The camera captures her blood-charged organ's pulsations in the pink shaded luster light. It anxiously thirsts to fornicate again. The heat from its recent carnal craving radiates palpably from the screen. It brazenly mocks the wife's inadequate mons' bramble-thicket and her notions about pious morality. The on-screen vagina defiantly displays what her husband craves.

"The wife gulps hard, as if her act of swallowing might end her husband's obsession with the craven, semen-spackled peach. Before seeing this film, her husband's attraction to Marty's immoral wantonness was incomprehensible. But now, after observing the peach's earnest passion while making love; seeing it, after fornicating, craving even more cocks, she finally understands.

"The gravitas of the wife's predicament weighs heavily upon her heart. It torments her. She again pays close attention to the passing film frames. Chortling, sin- obsessed Marty flaunts her iniquitous pleasures to the wife's listening ears. It strikes the wife that Marty's bantering with her lovers is purposely taunting her; mocking her sense of decency. The wife knows she cannot change Marty's immoral ways. She doesn't even know how to contact Marty. She hopped she

might dissuade her husband. But, after paying closer attention to the film, she knows she'll never overcome Marty's allure.

"The wife has a sudden epiphany. She realizes something profound. Marty is not like other women. Marty is not even like other porn stars. There's a uniqueness about Marty. The wife appreciates that uniqueness now. Marty's revelry reveals it. Destroying marriages is Marty's favorite sport! The wife now perceives that Marty's goal is to separate her husband from his moral moorings.

"Another epiphany grips the wife! It's the sensation that overwhelmed sanity at Salem's Massachusetts Colony! She sees everything clearly: Marty, the wife suddenly believes, is a witch! She witnessed Marty's eyes flinging her immoral poisoned darts at her heart. That confirmed it. Her new conviction rationalizes her misfortune.

"Like thunderclap booms in rapid succession, the wife has a third epiphany. Marty is not an ordinary porn star. And Marty is not an ordinary witch. No! Horrors! She is worse. She draws millions of men. They blindly join her journey to perdition. She gathers loyal flocks of sinners. Marty is the living Antichrist! She personifies the devil's flesh on Earth. She embodies all that is evil. The wife is overpowered. She knows it's impossible to retrieve her husband. He worships the Marty Devil. He seeks to become her sex slave. Everything is obvious! Marty's butterfly winged sex peach is her husband's god!

"The wife's only remaining recourse is to lash out; and thusly preserve morality's status quo. She must tear the poisoned darts from her heart and rid her life of Marty. But she cannot attack the film. It only delivers Marty's images. Real-life Marty is unassailable. The wife doesn't even know where Marty lives. She intuits that Marty has security. Separating Marty from her husband leaves her no choice. She must attack her husband. He sits before her, obsessing over Marty's irresistible eroticism. The wife summons her fury. She attacks her

husband with the vengeance of lightning strikes. A fight ensues. The wife harms her husband, perhaps fatally.

"Who caused this fight, Bertie? Surely, the wife will blame Marty. We'll also be blamed for the wife's madness. We won't be spared."

Bertie had far too much invested in her commitment to Marty to retreat from George's challenge. She was not having his objections. She defended her plan:

"George, don't be so negative. You are presuming that Marty and our film work intervened in that couple's love life and caused this harm; but who is to say that is the right way to look at it? We can't be responsible for the effect our art has on peoples' minds. We can only put our work out there. We can't go crazy trying to change our work to suit some imaginary persons' ideas of what is acceptable for them to watch. That's God's work and I won't interfere with it. We have the right to produce our films. Anyway, George, times have changed

"In pagan times, wives felt profoundly honored and blessed that their husbands consorted with temple prostitutes. There was no shame in prostitution worship. There was only honor to the temple. Womenfolk felt wonderful and secure, knowing that their family was right with the temple. Then, along came traditional western religions. Those faiths interfered with humanity's natural creation by conception worship. Right and wrong became defined in righteous, misogynistic-ordered distortions.

"The misogynists tipped their hand in The Book of Numbers, Chapter seven, George. If you study the text, you will see the verse numbers are coded references to solfeggio frequencies which, in the lower 258, 369, 417 frequencies and their variations, are the basis for Gregorian chanting. The higher ordered solfeggio frequencies are omitted, presumably because male voices cannot reach those high notes. And most women can't reach all the lower frequencies."

"Where are you going with this, Bertie?" George failed to see the relevance of Bertie's digression on the task of marketing Marty. *"Is this an extension of your 'misogynistic bearded homosexual goat fuckers taking power from women' theory?"*

"No, George. This is more profound than that. The goat boys were an oral tradition. When their tales got committed to writing, there was a mystical, ethereal style tone to those writings. The Book of Numbers was written in a separate, distinctive style. It's more rap, rap, rap; more martial, the opposite of the stochastic randomness, wandering narratives in the rest of the Hebrew Torah. Numbers was measured information dissemination. It was a calculated and coded messaging text. And it was about taking power and control. It's genius is that it used repetition of verse text to signal the verse numbers. Those numbers were reduced to code. Like a verse 28 became a two plus eight, or a ten, or a one plus zero, becomes a one; a verse 23 became a two plus three, or a five; a verse 17 became a one plus seven, or an eight; and so on. The next level of genius was how the encoded numbers form series that repeat, like 369, 258, 417, and so on. This layering of solfeggio frequencies in the coding of the text is not random, George. There's nothing stochastic about that Book. It's code for how to control women. It's in the Hebe's Torah for a reason. I believe it has to do with the 'God's Chosen People' concept."

"So, who wrote the coded text and why?"

"That, dear George, is a problematic question. Whoever it was, we know who it was not. It was not some goat herder looking at constellations and cooking up fairy tales. It was an intelligent being that understood the mathematics of harmonics and the powers of resonance. Perhaps, particularly, resonance powers in water, since our bodies hold a lot of water? Not sure about that; but the chants that can come from the combinations of solfeggio frequencies can be used to create certain moods; moods that can be sort of hypnotizing and useful for crowd control, especially in a religious, worshipping way."

"But who would know this stuff in the first place?"

"My guess, George: The same person(s) who messed with human DNA and experimented with DNA splicing where they encoded serpent DNA into our amygdala and pineal glands for our flight or fight commands and our sense of sleep and awake times."

"And these were the same people who coded some women to become nymphomaniac fuck bunnies, right?"

"That's right, George! Very good! I think they were the same people. They were creating a human population that would multiply and that could be controlled so that it would advance and accomplish wonders. And they wanted one tribe of humans, the Hebes, to be the leaders of this enlightened species. The coded frequencies were a key tool that enabled control. Remember, religious faith is key to making a population subservient to what the leaders want."

"Okay, I'm sort of getting this. But where did Moshe (Moses) and his followers first learn of these frequencies and their significance? Did they get them from the Egyptians? Perhaps from a lost civilization that predated Egypt? What happened to those people? Did the Earth have a sudden tectonic plate shift? Were entire continents suddenly subducted into Earth's mantle? How did knowledge of sacred geometric harmonic frequencies survive the cataclysm? And why did the survivors omit the higher ordered frequencies from their coded numerical messaging in the Book of Numbers? And why did the Catholic Church keep the higher frequencies concealed and use only male- friendly lower frequencies in its Gregorian chants?"

"I think it was the Anunnaki people, or their ruler person, whoever that was. I think they were here for thousands of years. I think they diddled human women, breeding with us until we all became the same physical size. They started off as large people and we started off as small people. But over thousands of years, we've all become more or less similar sized."

"But why did they want to breed with human women?"

"For the same reason today's men want to breed with us, George; because we are very beautiful and very sexy! Isn't that right, Marty?"

"Yes," giggled Marty. *"We are very beautiful and very sexy, don't you think, George?"*

"Of course, you are. You are all beautiful femme fatales," George leaned into Marty and kissed her cheek, then he looked at Bertie. *"But my question, Bertie, is this: Why did the Book of Numbers only encode the lower frequencies?"*

"Control, George. Men can't reach the higher frequencies. And most women can't reach the lowest frequencies. Only males could chant. Only males could form a minion to worship. Only males could sit close to the altar. Women needed to cover themselves and sit in the back of the portable temple tent. Only males could become priests. There was no female Bat Mitzvah. That came thousands of years later, like women's suffrage. You males have perfected ways of keeping women subjugated to your controls. In the days of the Anunnaki and the millennia that followed those ways were codified in the Book of Numbers. There was a male power grab to wrest away control of tribal leadership from women. And you males have tried your best to extinguish natural prostitution worship; but we women are making a comeback!

"We will take our rightful, natural power back, George. 'We will really rock you' is a solfeggio chant, George. Football fans in Kansas City understand its power. That's why their team plays great football. I'm going to run with my convictions, George. Everything natural and good and beautiful was swept aside by those ancient power grabbers. They insisted there was a god in heaven, sitting on a big throne chair. They assured people they would go to hell if they didn't do as they were told. They told the people that they were the only ones who knew what God wanted.

"But they were blowing smoke, George. The real power of creation is in the female vagina. The female vagina is beautiful, George.

It allures. It gives a sensuous feeling. It produces life. It tops what the male religious cults are pushing. Our deal, the female deal, is impossible to beat. I know it and they know it. It frightens the male religious types that we women will rise up and challenge those charlatans and upset their control games.

"So, getting back to your hypothetical example, I ask you, George, does not the religious beliefs of your imaginary porn-viewing wife and her church distort the natural order of things? Are they not the real culprits that caused her hurt? Come on, George, who's to say that some ancient tribal priests didn't decide to control their people by replacing the temple whores with sacrificial animals? Why was that okay in the first place? What about the animals? Who gave those priests the right to kill them? Who is to say that those priests weren't power crazed misogynist homosexuals that wrested control from the prostitutes who first controlled the tribes through natural prostitution worship? Marty and her New Morality Standard represent women pushing back, George. Think about that, George! Surely you can't believe that consenting adults, doing what comes naturally, caused your theoretical wife her hurts. Can you, honestly?"

George relented. He had to admit Bertie was right. They had solid defenses for their new business. He also relished being tasked to work with Marty. *"I suppose not. I can see that creating addiction to Marty and her vagina is similar to branding cigarettes or cars. But why do you believe women feel a need to push back against the established world order?"*

Bertie didn't hesitate. Her mission was commanded by the spirit world. It was unassailable. *"BECAUSE, GEORGE, THAT BUTERFLY TOLD ME SO!"* Bertie's jaw was set. Her face turned red. Her raised voice let George know she was losing patience. *"We're reasserting women's natural power, George. Between women's legs lies an irresistible magnetism. It's stronger than church services and orchestral music. It's time women reasserted it, and it's time for you men to fuck off!"* Bertie's voice softened. Doe-eyed and smiling warmly, she won George to her cause.

"Okay, Bertie, I'm in." George relented. He knew better than to fight when Bertie flared signs of anger. Yielding earned him later rewards. *"I understand morality is subjective. Those concerns should not stop us. But how are we going to make Marty's intimate artistry universally accepted? How will we create a cult of pagan prostitution worshippers?"*

IMAGE WORK

Tis beauty calls, and glory leads the way. (Nathaniel Lee: The Rival Queens)

Beauty is nature's coin, must not be hoarded.... Beauty is nature's brag and must be shown... (John Milton: Comus)

"By obeying the epiphany, I received from that butterfly, George." Bertie's tone softened. Anxieties melted. George was won over. *"It will happen because of our efforts. We'll follow the commands of the Great Spirit of all Living Things as spoken to me by the Spirit's messenger butterfly, George. The Spirit wants Marty and her beautiful artistry to be the foundation stone of a new world order. We will challenge the misogynistic order of things.*

"We've been tasked to craft Marty's image. We'll be her devoted disciples. We'll spread her gospel of divine pagan worship. We'll convince the world of the righteousness of immorality's cause. She'll become the high priestess of uninhibited erotic purity. We'll fashion her brand image as the most beautiful, ultimate immoral goddess, the divine personification of shameless uninhibited intimate artistry!

"How, you ask? By working on Marty's beautification to make her even more beautiful than she already is; by working on her techniques to make them even more alluring than they already are; by

working on her scripts, her lines, her motions and positioning on her screen sets; the designs of the sets she performs on; the lightings and camera angles that accentuate her face, her eyes, her mouth, her breasts, her lady lips; by perfecting the voice tones, enunciation, inflections and volumes of her spoken lines; by doing similar work with her film partners; by leaving no detail to chance. Nothing about Marty's films will look amateurish, awkward, or unprofessional in any way. They will be highly polished perfection masterpieces. Our superstar queen of romantic eroticism will have a refined, perfected image.

"We'll also mange her media image, George. When she seduces a famous person, we'll make sure a tabloid captures exclusive photos of the secret tryst. We'll help the tabloid blow up the man's marriage in exchange for gushing write-ups about Marty's sensational erotica scenes in her latest film. We'll relentlessly work every angle, George. We'll make Marty front page news. Her name will be on everyone's lips."

Marty loved what she heard. Why wouldn't she? Bertie was committed to promoting her career; and inviting Marty to share her bed with her and her husband. Her confident fingers tightened their grip and quickened their strokes on George's penis. Bertie continued:

"Trust me, George. This won't be hard for me. It will be my greatest joy. Marty already has voices within her spirit-self that encourage her to be promiscuous, shameless, and iniquitous. Those voices are her spirit soul. They tell her it's perfectly normal to be immoral; and that it is wonderful to do immoral things. Her natural immorality affects those who see her performances. They react to her immorality in ways that they believe will please her. There are silent, causative communications between her limbic zone and the limbic zones of her viewers. She awakens magical immoral connectivity in her fans. Her messaging assures them that immorality is good; healthy, and

beautiful. And her viewers delight in these communications. Human nature is working with us, George. Compare that to religious theologies. Human nature works against them. Their message tells their flocks to resist nature. Marty's message tells her followers to embrace nature."

"Do you honestly think she's unique, Bertie? There are thousands of women performing porn, you know. What makes you so confident that you can differentiate Marty's work from all the others?"

Bertie bristled. *"George, don't ever question my judgment. That butterfly appeared to me for a reason. I didn't fully understand its message at first; but now, after watching Marty's films, I know what I'm seeing. I understand my purpose in life. It's to enhance the lust effect which Marty creates in millions of men and women. It's to recreate in men's minds the same feeling a little boy experiences when he is smitten with his first love.*

"Suddenly that little girl who admired his frogs and snakes; who watched birds with him, is no longer just another buddy. Some causative phenomenon happens inside the mental chemistries of that little girl and that little boy. Cupid's arrow strikes. It finds the boy. He falls head over heels in love with the girl. Before that moment, she was just ordinary. She happened to be one of the guys. But now, in his mind and body chemistry, that little girl is transformed.

"She becomes angelic. She's beautiful beyond any words he can find to describe her; even with popped bubble gum smeared all over her face. He can't get enough of her; can't be with her long enough; and can't do enough for her. He wants to walk her to school, and back home. He begs to carry her school books. He takes her to his favorite fishing hole, yielding the one secret he never showed the other boys. He shows off and acts goofy around her; tries to make her laugh. He knows when she laughs, she's happy; and he wants her to be happy. He climbs trees, races other boys to show her that he's a superior boy. He helps her do her chores; everything to prove his worthiness.

"He'll carry a two by three-inch photo of her school picture in his shirt pocket, so his heart is close to her image. He steals flowers from a neighbor's yard to give her a small bouquet. When he sits with his parents in church, he doesn't hear a word the preacher says. Instead, he steals glances at her. He adores her face, her lips, and eyes; the way her hair looks. In short, yesterday she was just there; today thoughts of her consume him. It's puppy love. It's infatuation. It's obsession. But nothing else in the world matters. He dreams of her. She's his whole world."

Ever so subtly, Marty began applying downward pressure while stroking George's penis through his pants. The effect on George was large. He yearned for this session to end. His thoughts took him forward, imagining he was making love with Marty, trying to rationalize the unfamiliar world into which he was falling:

'Marty is young enough to be my daughter. How can I be her lover and not think of my lost daughter? And, if I push my memories of my child from my mind, am I not betraying her father's love? Am I not denying my grief? Am I seeing Marty as my daughter now, instead of my child; as if my child never lived? And if I imagine I'm making love with my daughter, is that not incest? Am I not the most despicable sinner of sinners? But, with Marty, it could not be incest, could it? She's not my daughter. And she's had lovers; some from her Premium Service are older than me. I wouldn't contaminate her life. I wouldn't cause her psychological problems. She loves making love. She is, after all, a working girl. I'd disappoint her if I didn't perform with her. But I know I will fall in love with her. I already have.

'How will she think of me? Will I be her porn prop; nothing more? Her Sugar Daddy? Bertie has already committed me to bequeathing her all our worldly wealth; already given her keys to the west wing of our mansion; already told her to feel free to live here with us; and bring Bob, too. Bertie already told her to feel free to entertain her porn partners in our home, use our pool, our movie studio, and

tennis courts. We already treat her like she's our daughter. But, she's completely different from our daughter. My little girl was good, pure, moral; a sweet innocent child. Marty looks the part of purity and innocence; but she's the opposite of those qualities. So, what will I be to this vixen? Her scratching post when she's angry about something or someone? Her quick fix when she has an itch? Her porn-prop? Sugar Daddy? Incestuous lover? Old fool? Overaged boy-toy? Confidant? All of the above? What will I be, really?

'Why am I agreeing to this? It's Bertie. It's all about Bertie. It was never about our daughter. I told Bertie she should train our girl at the rink where a paramedic was always on duty. But, no, Bertie rejected that. She wanted the freedom of that open space ice; those hard, full throttle power runs. It was never about our baby or her safety. It was about Bertie's manic need to boss our child and me. It was about Bertie's manic ego to prove she could create the best performer in the world; about Bertie taking credit for whipping a human being into a perfect performer. Bertie always bullies me. I never stand up to her. Now? Why bother? My baby is gone. I have nothing left. No pride, no self-respect, no will to fight Bertie over her latest obsession.

'Bertie is a psychological monster. There's no use trying to change her or even pointing out her madness to her. I suppose I'll just go along for the ride. After all, screwing this juicy porn star will be a treat for my libido. I know I'm rationalizing what I'm about to do. But there's no percentages in fighting it.

'Maybe, just maybe, Bertie will meet her match in Marty. Our daughter never could stand up to Bertie; but Marty doesn't have that natural mother-daughter bond. The two of them may pretend to have it; but they don't. There's no blood tie between them. Maybe Marty will wake up one day from her play dream and tell Bertie she's had enough. Maybe Marty will be the one to take down Bertie's ego. I'll watch, see how this unfolds. But I cannot imagine Marty

standing on a stage, accepting all the awards for being the world's most famous adult film star; and then saying that it is all thanks to Bertie. She wouldn't do that because that would send her competition to Bertie for training. So, rather than me being the one to blow up Bertie's fantasy, I'll just play along and wait. I suspect the day will come when Marty derails Bertie's manic train ride. The young minx will tell her where to get off. I'll wait this out. It should be fascinating.'

Bertie had continued talking:

"George, what I sense is that the same causative chemistry that suddenly bonded together that young girl and that young boy works between Marty and grown men as well. By whatever twist of fate, Marty uniquely captured her little girl chemistry and retained it in her adult persona. And her chemistry has never diminished. It has increased! Marty naturally holds out the same rapture appeal to millions of grown men that that little girl holds out to that love-smitten little boy. Like that love-struck little boy, men's' minds become altered by Marty's persona and image. Their reasoning ability operates on a limbic level, instead of on a rational level."

"It's called sex appeal, Bertie." George reclaimed his musings and returned to the present. He and Marty chuckled. Marty squeezed her hand tightly on George's penis, signaling her agreement with Bertie's assessments; then, she relaxed her squeeze and continued stroking, casually and with appreciation of George's vulnerability to her.

Bertie continued: *"Men adore Marty in that same emotive way as the little boy adores the little girl; and they wish only good things, good times, and endless happiness for Marty. Like the boy, they are willing to go to great lengths to please Marty. In their eyes, Marty can do no wrong."*

FIRST MURDER, FIRST SEX

"That's so true, Bertie," interrupted Marty.

"I was home from WEX for two months during the summer after my first school year. A boy named Kenny lived down the street from Mother's house. We were both six years old. Kenny and I were playing in his back yard when he showed me his garden snake and his toad. He asked me if I'd kiss his snake. I said: 'Sure.' He held it down while I knelt on the ground and kissed its head. He wanted me to kiss his toad, too. I told him I didn't like toads and I wouldn't kiss his toad. I told him I wanted him to kill it. He said toads ate bugs and his dad said they were good for their garden.

"I told him I didn't care that his toad ate bugs. I hated the toad because it was ugly. I told him we should kill it. He said he wouldn't kill it; but we could take it to the edge of the forest and let it go. I told him it would just come back if we let it go; so, we should kill it. He said he wouldn't kill it; but if I wanted to kill it, he'd be okay with that. I told him I needed something sharp to stick through the toad to kill it. He went into his house and came back with a pencil. I took his pencil and stuck it through his toad. We watched the toad struggle. It crawled around and struggled with the pencil stuck through it. It moved in a circle and wasn't getting anywhere; but it wouldn't die.

"After a while, I got tired of watching the toad crawling around and not dying, so I decided I needed to bash its head with a rock. I picked up a rock from their garden and held the pencil so the toad couldn't move. Then I bashed its head a few times until it stopped moving. I had finally killed it.

"Kenny was shocked. He looked at me like he was a little afraid of me. He asked me how I could kill the toad like that. I told him I killed it because Mother made me go to WEX School and I was angry about that; and I was still upset about losing my dad and my dog. I told him it was easy to kill the toad once I made up my mind

to kill it. Then he asked me if I liked him because he let me kill his toad. I told him: 'Yes.' Then he asked if he could kiss me. I told him: 'Yes,' again. He kissed me on my lips. Then he asked me if he could kiss me some more; and I said: 'Yes,' again.

"We went into Kenny's basement and took our shorts off. Kenny kissed me a few times on my lips. Then he asked me if he could kiss my vagina. I didn't understand what he meant; so, Kenny explained that my vagina was my girl thing. He told me his boy thing was called a pecker. I told him he could kiss my vagina if he wanted. He knelt down and kissed my vagina three times, like he had kissed me on my lips. He didn't try to put his tongue inside me. I pulled on his penis several times. I noticed it was hard. I was about to kiss his pecker, just like I had kissed his snake. But then we heard his mother upstairs, so we left his place and went to my backyard. Mother was away seeing Marvin. Kenny and I swinged on my backyard swing set a while.

"Then Kenny asked me if I thought we had sex. I told him I was pretty sure that we did. He asked me if that was my first time for sex, and I told him it was. He asked me if I liked having sex and I told him I did. Then he told me he loved me and said he would love me for the rest of his life. He told me I was beautiful. That was the first time a boy told me I was beautiful. I felt kind of funny hearing him say that. I realized that I had some kind of power over him because he thought I was beautiful.

"He said he loved me because I wasn't afraid to be bad and because I let him have sex with me. He said watching me kill his toad made him admire me for being so sure of myself. He said it excited him and made him want to do whatever I told him to do; and it made him want to kiss me and follow me anywhere and bring me presents. That was my first inkling that boys liked bad girls more than they liked good girls; and that they would reward girls for being bad girls.

"Then he said he needed to go home to get his pencil and bury his toad. Before he left, he asked me if he could see me and have sex with me again. I told him: 'Yes; I'd like that.' I never saw him again."

Bertie chuckled:

"There you have it. That's what I'm talking about. Marty's immorality was acceptable to that boy. Men are boys at heart. They see Marty in the same way that little boy saw her. Whatever she does is perfectly acceptable. They approve. They expect her to be bad. They admire her badness. And they love her for it. They see her whoring as a natural expression of her persona. They approve of her promiscuous conduct, no matter how lewd. They see her immoral film performances as a morally good thing, because they intuit that the act of creating her films pleased her, like killing that toad pleased her. They view her demolition of marriages, even their own, as nothing more than sporting contests.

"They subconsciously cheer for Marty to murder the spirit souls of her pesky rival wives. Her Premium Members cheer Marty while she executes her coup de grace: the dipping of their wedding rings into her semen pool; signaling the final murder of their marriages. In their eyes, Marty is a beautiful goddess. Whatever pleases her; whatever enhances her seductress image, makes them immensely happy; especially watching her passion lusting during her orgies and threesomes.

"They need to know Marty's libido is happy and satisfied. They psychologically commit themselves to further her happiness. That adoration drives their lives. Grown men rediscover those same obsessive feelings they had as love smitten little boys. Like little boys, they also act on these feelings. They had to pick those flowers and carry those books for that little girl. They likewise feel compelled to buy Marty's films. Their limbic impulse driver is that same boyhood quest that drives them to acquire the top baseball card. It's the same as their desire for a hot sports car. Now, it's Marty. They obsess over

her. *They write her letters and send her gifts. Some send gratuitous money tips after watching her films. They include messages telling her that they love what she does.*

"They feel the same rapture awe that little Kenny felt while he watched Marty kill his toad. Some praise her performance in a particular scene. Others wax enthusiastic over a climactic visual, where she casually flows semen from her vagina. They imagine the semen stream was theirs, and inquire about making that become reality. Some feel a duty to join her Premium Service. This seems like Neanderthal madness to academics who study male behavior. But to men enraptured by Marty, it's reality.

"They feel unbounded rapture while she experiences her orgasms. They feel adoration flood their libidos while she seduces new lovers. Their limbic zones want her happiness, wellbeing, and wealth accumulation. Her fans are protective of her. She can do nothing wrong. Her bad is their good. Like smitten little boys, they fixate on her. She's the one they love, idolize, and cherish.

"This is different from the self-gratification they feel while watching other porn stars. They view, abstractedly, while those lesser porn stars are ravaged during orgies. They have no empathy for them; no identification with their pleasures or the pleasures they give their partners. It's different with Marty. They identify WITH her; feel what SHE feels. They vicariously imagine how wonderfully she feels when a cock first penetrates her vaginal lips. Upwelling love pours from their souls while they observe her joyfully making love."

"They love knowing she's her happiest while she's fucking, right?" George cast a mischievous smile toward Marty. She nodded meekly while repeatedly squeezing and releasing her grip on his cock.

"Yes, they certainly do, George," Bertie nodded her assurance.

"Think in terms of an iconic brand, George. When people decide they want to smoke, they associate smoking with their brand. It

could be a cowboy riding a horse, for example. When they think of drinking a bear or a soda, they associate their drink with a particular brand, right? They don't just go to the store shelf and grab the first drink that's there. They look until they locate the brand that's in their minds. It's the same with buying a car or an over-the-counter medication. People search out their brands.

"Well, many people watch pornography, George. Sex sells. So, we must differentiate Marty's artistry and associate it with the logo of her vagina's butterfly wings and her eyes. We'll work on that. We'll convince viewers that her eyes are the windows into her soul. Their souls can enter hers by looking into her eyes. Her butterfly wings will direct them into her pleasure channel. If they seek pleasure, they need to buy products labeled with her butterfly wings. Are you understanding me, George?"

"Yes. I get it. Place the product in their minds. Position and promote her wings and eyes. Marty's Monarch butterfly wings will trademark her vagina. Why the Monarch? It's the king of butterflies. Marty's vagina is the vagina for a king. Get it?"

"Okay. Yes. We can run with that." George nodded. Marty squeezed harder. She never had a marketing team before. She loved what Bertie was saying.

Bertie noted what they had to work with: *"Marty's fans already reciprocate the pleasures she gives them. They eagerly buy more films, not only because those films satisfy their curiosity, but also because they believe it pleases Marty when they buy her work. When she releases a film, they hear a call to duty; and they buy. They are habitually addicted to Goddess Marty.*

"Some leave their wives to join Marty's Premium Service; not only to please themselves by cavorting with her; but by surrendering to her, pleasing her. That's addiction. They buy her films and join her service because they LOVE her. They NEED to please her. That's the addiction. They live life in adoration of her, much like priests live

in adoration of God. They are smitten little boys over their first true love.

"We will build on those followers' attraction, George. Instead of thousands of followers, Marty will have millions. She'll become known as Queen Goddess of Whoredom: Superstar of Promiscuity; Purveyor of Shameless Immorality. She'll be the ultimate authority on wantonness. We'll condition her fans to adore her wanton behavior and affairs. We'll make her the world's arbiter of The New World Order of Immorality. And, she'll lead by example.

"She'll challenge accepted orthodoxies. People will love her for it. They'll hang onto every word she speaks; mimic everything she does. I know people, George. They like being led. They need to be led. They do not lead. They follow. Marty will lead as their goddess of socially acceptable norms. Her fans will cheer when she destroys a famous married couple or seduces a new trophy partner. People will congregate wherever she appears. They'll buy her movies and branded merchandise. She'll be a phenomenon. Political and religious leaders will seek her audience to learn her views. She'll change world opinions!"

"Bertie, you say she has special internal chemistry. Why is she special? Doesn't everyone have that same chemistry?"

Hearing the question, Marty pinched George's penis with her thumb and forefinger, letting him know her chemistry was indeed special. His hardness spoke volumes. He was ready for sex. She continued stroking, as if to let him know she nevertheless respected his question, while listening attentively to Bertie.

"No, they don't George. I'm not talking about chemical chemistry. It's chemistry of the spirit soul. Marty's is unique. Her innermost persona believes that her immoral acts are pure and innocent. She feels divinely inspired to be immoral. She thinks her immorality is a social goodness, don't you Marty?" Marty smiled at Bertie and nodded, continuing, unashamedly, to stroke George's penis.

"She feels no wrongdoing while cannibalizing a marriage, do you, dear?"

Marty smiled meekly, shaking her head to let Bertie know she concurred. She harbored no sense of wrongdoing or immodesty while comfortably stroking George's penis. *"She feels she's doing something glorious and good while performing an orgy or a three-some. That's her spirit chemistry. That's why sweet serenity radiates from her face. It's why sparkling joy in her loving eyes leaps out at you while she receives an ejaculation and when she welcomes a penis into her vagina. Making pornography causes you no feelings of shame or embarrassment whatsoever, does it dear?"* Bertie turned her question to Marty.

Marty replied. *"No, Bertie, none whatsoever. It's exhilarating. I never feel ashamed of what I'm doing."*

Bertie appreciated Marty's confirmation.

"See, George! There you have it. Marty is proud of her work. She internalizes that pride. It's work she enjoys. She cherishes, adores, and celebrates it. That's what presents us with this great opportunity, George. Her spirit soul, combined with the way men obsess over her, observing the sweet innocent purity of her smile while performing immoral acts gives us our perfect product. We can and will develop Marty into the world's most sensational sex goddess. We'll create enormous, insatiable demand for her. We'll change the world, George."

George looked into Marty's eyes.

"You'll be de Monde: The World!" he smiled lovingly to her. Then, turning to Bertie: *"You're obsessed over her, aren't you?"*

"Yes, George, I admit it. I'm in love with her, as I see you are. I'm drowning in my obsession. It's a good place for me, George. Don't try to rescue me. I don't want to be pulled out of it. I want to drown in it. I want to immerse myself in Marty's world. I want to be at her side as I create a brand image and a world for her.

"I want people to see her as a divine goddess, sent to them to see how inspired women's sexual needs are; how there's nothing immoral about those needs; and how glorious it is to have those needs fulfilled. I want our films to communicate divine inspiration. I want the entire world to love and adore Marty, the same way many feel about religion."

"But she represents sin and immorality. She's the opposite image of religion." George felt he needed to mention the discrepancy in Bertie's logic.

"Religious practices can differ greatly between beliefs and over time, George." Marty interjected. Hearing George say she was the opposite of religion challenged her sense of self worth.

"I know, George," Bertie ignored Marty's comment. *"And that's our challenge. We need to work hard to bring about this revelation. We need to change the way the world thinks about explicit erotica. We need to help them appreciate it as divinely inspired art; and we need to help them feel it's okay to love it. We need to help them see immorality as good; sweet and innocent; the opposite of how they see immorality now. And we need to encourage them to love and adore our Marty."*

"You said you love her. You love her even more than you love me, don't you, Bertie?"

George glanced first a look to Marty, then a taunting look to his wife. His eyes knew the future that Bertie's determination would create. Young Marty would rise in stardom and blossom into the Empress of Erotica. Bertie would be her agent, publicist and guiding mentor, lighting the way for the younger woman to become the Queen of all Whoredom. Bertie would remove the stigma of pornography; refashion it into explicit intimate erotica for a world that was bifurcating into those with money who could afford the finest courtesans of sensual indulgences, and into those who could only dream of such pleasures.

George's gaze stayed level and fixed on Bertie, implying there was more he wished to say but feared to hear the truth of Bertie's honest reply. Her truthful eyes confirmed all he needed to know. Bertie was to become Marty's most ardent and faithful lover in a new, flexible sharing arrangement with Bob and Marty's other occasional love interests.

Then something occurred to him. Something wasn't quite right about Bertie's intended arrangement. Perhaps it was a stray figment of his imagination. Maybe his gut was trying to express something it intuited through some fleeting telepathy escaping from the vixen that found its way to him. He wanted to ask Bertie whether she should slow things down a bit; hire someone to run a thorough check on Marty. Something sparked in his thoughts that the young porn star's immorality might encompass more than her whoring and adulterous liaisons. It suddenly occurred to George that Marty might hurt Bertie somehow.

But his logical mind quickly brushed his premonition aside. He told himself he was simply feeling petty jealousy over losing Bertie, his comfortable love; and trying to forestall Bertie's inevitable surrender to her lust for the young star. He told himself that, although thoroughly immoral, Marty was pure of heart; and she'd never harm a friend and benefactor.

'No,' he thought. *'She'd never do anything untoward.'*

He recalled how Marty's eyes shined with joyous satisfaction after her sensational fellatio coaxed fabulous ejaculations from her lovers onto her tongue and over her breasts. He gauged the wholesomeness of her victorious smile. It had a certain winsome healthy confidence about what she was able to accomplish with her mouth and fingers. It was sincere and pure; disarming; filled with pride over how she coaxed surrendered semen from those penises. Effervescence for life glowed in her rosy cheeks when those cocks confessed their adoration.

She had paused momentarily, as if reflecting upon her triumph; and then, as if to honor the penises for their choice to shower her with their essences, she, one by one, kissed and stroked each of them a while longer. She lived her nirvana. She loved herself and everything she did with those penises. It was inspiring and beautiful. He basked in her innocence. How could he harbor any thought other than happiness for her pleasure? She was the essence of honest purity, completely assured in the rightness of her immorality. Her face beamed like a proud farm girl's who had just won grand prize at the county fair.

George saw that behind Marty's beautiful face and body there was a woman with an incredibly perceptive mind and sense of purpose. She had an instinctive emotive intelligence and a determination to live life on her own terms; beholden to no one. As long as he and Bertie did not oppose her, they had no cause for concerns. He reasoned:

'I understand Marty's character. Immorality, intimate artistry, whatever you choose to call it, are simply her chosen venue. She has no use for conformists. She is anything but. Politics, religion, rules, and causes hold no appeal for her, except the notion that a woman should have complete freedom, including mental freedom, to enjoy her sexuality.'

George had heard Marty's history. The loss of her father; her mother's indifference and abandonment; her experimentations with sex; her grandmother's religious bent; her mother's rejection of her grandmother's values. It was all clear to him. Marty had climbed the ladder of self-actualization in search of stability, self worth, perhaps a connection to God; and ultimately a desire to share with others the joys of sexual freedom she had discovered in her own life.

Every authority figure in Marty's life: her teachers, swim coach, especially her shrinks, had merely used her. They pushed her along without helping her find the inner peace she sought. Marty was forced to discover her own path to fulfillment and belief in a higher power. It all started when she was a little girl convincing herself that the stones loved her when no one else would. She needed love and somehow convinced herself that inert stones loved her. That abstract love was enough for Marty, until she met Maria. Their brief lesbian relationship unleashed Marty's sexuality and shattered the inhibitions demanded by her grandmother's religion. From delicious lesbianism with Maria, Marty quickly advanced to penises and experimentations with all forms of sex for pleasure. George visualized the young woman's life changes as they unfolded.

HER METAMORPHOSIS

And yet, as angles in some brighter dreams call to the soul when man doth sleep, so some strange thoughts transcend our wonted themes and into glory peep. (Henry Vaughn: They are all gone)

Marty appreciated a truth. We create our own fulfillments. She didn't need a higher power. She traversed that belief threshold; became her own Goddess. Her body was her temple. She assumed others who were trapped in failing belief systems may, as well, instead worship her. She had George and Bertie now. They adored and trusted her; supported her ambitions. Her tattoo boldly declared her belief system was Pagan. Her unapologetic whoring was the natural progression of that belief system. Her metamorphosis was almost complete.

Transforming Marty believed her immorality was normal, righteous behavior. That belief gave her serene confidence and breathtaking sexuality. It captivated George while he witnessed her exquisite fellatio. This belief was Marty's guiding light. It

became Satan's version of Paganism. She made no effort to conceal or mask this inner light. She let it shine. She believed in it;
enjoyed, and lived it. And she believed others should live pagan
lives as well. Awestruck George saw nothing wrong with Marty's
beliefs. She was transforming herself from a troubled child into
a confident woman. Was she not a reflection of what our materialistic world had fashioned? Who was he to say which life path
another's soul should take?

George chastised himself:

*'What's wrong with me? How can I have untoward thoughts
about her when every impulse I have is to sweep her up in my arms,
hold her close to me and hug her? She's darling. Is she not the most
beautiful, ravenous purveyor of fellatio I've ever seen? My skepticism
must be wrong. She is a gorgeous free-spirited woman who needs
to be loved for the adorable person she is. There is total honesty in
her. She's a pure sexual nymph, the personification of unapologetic
innocence. Can I not tell by her smile, the gleam in her eye, the cant
of her head and the lilt of her chin that she wholeheartedly believes
in the righteousness of her cause? Do I not see that her whole conscience being is devoted to lavishing irresistible pleasures upon the
male penis? Yes, there's a purity, an honest innocence, about the way
she goes about her lovemaking. It's natural; not contrived or learned.
I must accept her as she is. Bertie must be right. Her butterfly messenger delivered our truth to both of us.*

*'Who would I be to doubt her sincerity? What greater felicity
can any woman have than what Marty displayed in that film? Who
am I to judge her? Are not her publicity articles, her spoken words,
and her film craft all enshrouded in First Amendment protections?
And is not her professed faith of Satanic Pagan whoring also protected by the same First Amendment right to Freedom of Religion?
No one has a monopoly on those freedoms, do they? So, isn't Marty
simply enjoying her freedoms which our country's founding fathers*

intended us to enjoy? Isn't then our darling Marty the ultimate ideal citizen that the founding fathers sought to empower and protect? Of course! She personifies all of that; and so much more.

'She is a persona obsessed with spreading those freedoms of good will and love; not by sermonizing from a pulpit, but by spreading her legs! There's nothing objectionable about the way she proselytizes. I must respect who she is and the choices she has settled upon to enjoy and practice. They suit her temperament and inclinations perfectly. She needs all the encouragement and support I can possibly give her. Shame on me! How could I attribute a nefarious motive to her loving, beautiful face? I must love and adore her. And I will!'

George foresaw how his and Bertie's amour would end. Before Marty, he had assumed their souls would stay bonded together until one of them died. Death would bring about separation. But, with Amanda gone, things had changed. He saw that Bertie's soul would bind to Marty's. His own soul would flit-bounce between the souls of both women. It would attach to whomever needed him most, at that moment. It would be available for the times they needed him for their film practices. He resigned himself to losing his status as Bertie's only love. He rationalized that surrendering his place in Bertie's life in exchange for meeting the sexual demands of both women was not exactly condemnation to Hades.

All the pain of losing Amanda and their efforts to rekindle love had come to this. The traumatic shock of sudden loss, the stress of trying to go on living without precious little Mandy; the pretense that they could keep their illusory family intact, while knowing they couldn't, had finally delivered Bertie to her baseline. She needed to coach and shape a protégé. It was more than her reaction to losing her child. Bertie needed to have a cause that gave her life meaning. In Marty, Bertie discovered that cause.

Bertie also needed raw sexual love again, something she knew she could not recapture with George. How could she? How could any woman feel passion for a pair of old worn-out shoes, compared to a stylish new pair? George understood that love sputters and dies this way. Old loves fade. Their petals drop away and die. New loves bud, bloom fragrant, dazzle and beckon.

George knew the young sexpot had captured Bertie's passions. Bertie was moving on. She wouldn't actually leave him. She cared for him too much to do that. But she was fascinated by the young vixen now. She was head over heels infatuated. Marty's effervescent eroticism was Bertie's catnip. The young minx's iniquitous vagina was devouring Bertie's life. Marty had become Bertie's obsession.

George was familiar with Bertie's lesbian fascination. It was a fact of their lives together; but before it was only an occasional diversion, or so he was told. Now, the brutal truth was in Bertie's eyes, staring evenly at him. She loved the vixen minx. She wanted to become a love item with the juicy young bitch. She was even willing to subjugate both their lives to her new love. George tried to console himself. After all, he was slated to be their prop-penis practice toy. They'd take turns fucking him. It would be more than he could physically handle. But something would be gone. He would no longer be Bertie's professed love. That was over.

"Yes, George. I do love her more than I love you. I love her as if she were our own daughter, sent to us to discover the meaning of love and life again."

Bertie had finally answered his question. Her voice felt the pain she saw in George's eyes. He had always faithfully loved her to the depths of his soul. He was like her true companion dog. She couldn't put him down without saying consoling words. She still loved him, just not in the same way as the tasty morsel that preoccupied her mind. She knew she needed to be honest with him; and that, like a faithful dog, he'd understand.

"I've always been honest with you, George. I'll always love you, my sweet dumpling; but I love Marty more than my life itself; and I

would gladly give up my life; and yours, too, if that would increase her happiness in some way. I love her that much. I know I'm obsessed, but the pure innocence of her immorality melts my heart."

"Bertie, just listen to you! Where is this taking us?" George felt alarmed by Bertie's "and yours, too" quip.

"LISTEN to me George." Bertie bared her teeth, now revealing her sharpened voice. She did that when she became emphatically serious about something. *"I'm on to something here. Our marriage is not going to derail it, either. We ALL have this terrific opportunity."*

Bertie cleverly wrapped her love obsession in the blanket of a business opportunity. She knew she wouldn't fool George with this ploy; but she needed to do it anyway; easing her own conscience.

"I see our opportunity clearly. We're going to change the way men think about love. When we finish branding Marty, they will no longer think love means taking a walk or a hike with their woman; or going to dinner and a show with her. They will not even see their woman's smiling face in their minds. They won't even THINK about raising a family with her. Whenever they hear the word love, or even when they see some woman's legs or breasts, or lips, they are going to automatically think about Marty's delicious vagina, with its beautiful butterfly tattoo; with our color-hued lens' lighting perfectly showcasing it; and a huge penis eagerly waiting to penetrate it. We are going to make Marty's vagina synonymous with love, George; romantic erotic love.

"We're going to peel away all other forms of love from men's minds and train their minds to equate love with their fantasies of making love with Marty. We'll make men obsess over her face and body; her voice; her movements; her smile; her everything. She will be the superstar of sex, George. We're going to refashion love and romance to mean graphically explicit erotica, complete with slow motion and still frame viewing. The world is ready for it, George. I feel it in my gut. And we're going to push our Marty's

'EYES BEHIND THE BUTTERFLY ™' erotica brand, the way erotica should be experienced; by losing one's soul in it; affirming one's love of it.

"So, we're going to be doing lots of experiments with Marty, George; and when we're finished, we'll change the world."

Bertie's eyes glimpsed her distant vision. Her gleam saw and believed that the way the world had been ordered for the past six thousand years needed changing; turned all the way back, much like Hillary Clinton's red reset button, to that ancient time when women commanded tribal spiritual power over men. Women oversaw the temple altars. Women were the high priestesses. They were the ones receiving offerings, not for slaughtering animals for sacrifice, but for performing ritual prostitution services on their temple altars. There was nothing immoral about prostitution then. It was honored and revered. Prostitution was a holy sacrament; a beautiful covenant between the tribal family and the temple. Bertie believed her envisioned reversion was personified in Marty. She believed Marty was the divine gift that the Spirit had resurrected and offered to her. The spirit had communicated her vision through its messenger butterfly.

"Our brand will take back women's power that was stolen by the usurper priests. Our way is the better way. Consorting with free spirited women has always been glorious and fulfilling. It still is; now more than ever! It's the divine will of the Spirit, George. It's time, George. Women's time has returned! It's long overdue."

"Bertie, you just made me recall a dream I had. It was so real. I believe it actually happened." Marty suddenly became animated.

"Tell us, dear." Bertie's eyes widened. Her body posture became attentive.

"Well, I was a performing temple prostitute. There were, maybe twelve of us. It must have been about six thousand years ago. Suddenly these men in our tribe pulled out these daggers they had

concealed in their animal skins. They screamed at us. They were yelling that God was taking his revenge upon us; that we were vile blasphemers; that the true God was with them.

"They attacked us. They murdered nine of us; but I and two of the other women escaped into the forest. We watched what the men did to the prostitutes they had murdered. They threw their bodies into the temple fire and burned them like we always burned our tribal enemies. Then they declared that, from that time forward, the tribe would only sacrifice animals upon an altar to their One God. They said that from then on, prostitution worship was forbidden and punishable by death. Then, they smashed the statue of Baal, which resembled a huge penis.

"They said: 'From then on, men will pray to this new God before their altar, where they will sacrifice animals to it; and women will sit far behind the men at these new worship services, because women were not worthy enough to be close to the men or the altar.' These men who took over the tribe were very violent. Everyone feared and obeyed them. My two friends and I journeyed through the forest, looking for another tribe of Baal worshippers who might have mercy on us and take us in. Then, my dream ended."

"How did you feel about your dream, Marty?"

"Frightened. I woke up in a sweat. Bob told me I had screamed in my sleep. I sat there, in bed, terrified. I thought what I dreamed must have happened, for real, long ago. And I thought that these men, who had forced this new religion on our tribe. They were very authoritative, uncompromising, nasty, and ruthless, bad men. We were all so happy and loving. Life was so pleasant before those men came and did those terrible things."

"Who knows, Marty? Perhaps your DNA caused you to have a flashback? But maybe your dream was trying to tell us that it's natural and healthy to examine and sometimes revise humanity's concept of morality. Perhaps that's as needed as it is for the earth to

periodically reverse its magnetic poles. Otherwise, things become too rigid; too constrained.

"Regardless of why this has happened for us, George, the spirits have delivered Marty as their change agent. We're going to get so good at branding Marty's foo-foo that we'll be able to use it to sell merchandise and help people save fifteen percent on their car insurance! How does that sound, you big guy stud muffin?"

"So, there will be a money component to all this? Right, Bertie?"

"Of course, George, there's a money component to all religions. The Pope doesn't traipse about in rags, does he?"

"No, of course not. So, this will be a business venture?" George warmed to the idea. He was an exceptionally talented, natural salesman. Once sold on something himself, he was unstoppable.

"Yes. We'll test market our work with film productions. We'll emphasize what works best and we'll delete what doesn't. We'll optimize profit. We'll make Marty more than a sex symbol, George. She'll be a bigger than life, morality transformational goddess. We'll create Marty's image as humanity's approachable, good-to-know goddess, who helps you discover the beauty of immoral paganism; kind of like Christianity brands Jesus as their relatable guy who can get you closer to God. Marty will be seen as the fresh-faced, all-American girl next door, who also just happens to be a glamorous, lovable, uninhibited, totally immoral star of erotica films. We're going to fashion Marty's image as the universal symbol of love as WE redefine love to include romantic erotic love. Her brand image will sell, George. Trust me.

"I'm going to create a logo based on her butterfly tattoo, George. It will be a stunning, riveting logo that fires imaginations. It will stimulate emotions of intrigue, sexuality, and love. We'll promote that logo as the ultimate pathway to EROS. Print and video media marketing will make it synonymous with romantic, erotic love.

"We'll create a recognizable brand that people will buy. In these troubled times, everyone needs an escape, George; and the ultimate escape for everyone, no matter their age or sex, is passionate erotic love. They'll buy Marty's films, her branded jewelry, perfumes, clothing, and luggage. Why? Because when they make that transaction, they'll be acquiring love's image, that's why. They'll be making this statement: 'No one can take love from me. Love is who I am!'

"The world will idolize Marty, George. Whenever people see a butterfly, they'll think of Marty and her glorious freedom loving vagina; and love. Butterflies are erratic and spontaneous. They defy control, George. Love is also spontaneous. It also defies control. Marty defies control. Our logo will symbolize defiance of control. Every woman who purchases our brand will be stating that she defies being controlled; that she offers love; and that her quest for love can never be taken from her. Butterflies the world over will naturally promote our brand, George. They will heighten our brand awareness, whenever they flutter!"

"But, Bertie, governments give people benefits; religions give people hope. What can we GIVE them?"

"We'll give them the greatest thing in the world, George. We'll give them love; that irresistible desire from their limbic zones. Think of humanity's collective brain as a Ying and Yang thing, George. Male oriented religious orthodoxy has had a big run. The Ying now dominates; but it has run its course. It is weakening. The world and its institutions are losing their control of everything.

"Humanity's Yang is about to ascend. Religious immorality, led by Marty, is about to take control of the world, George. We'll help bring about this change. We'll commission sculptors to create statues and busts of Marty so she can be worshipped like a church icon. We'll hire artists and engravers to fashion gold and silver collectable coins with her face on one side and a seductive pose on the other. The coins and her exquisite seductive photos will promote

her love brand like baseball cards promote baseball. We'll keep the mental image of Marty and her fabulous vagina ever present, everywhere. We'll use our contacts, George. We'll have them write testimonials about how Marty's films helped their libido. We'll have our media reporters advocate that her films should be given Academy Awards. We'll create more than a fad, George. We'll create a change in world culture."

Dawn broke in George's mind. He had his own epiphany. Bertie wasn't going through all this effort, only to fashion Marty into the world's number one porn star. She had a far bigger goal. Bertie sought nothing less than to remake the way the world's power structure was ordered. She wanted to reverse power polarities; reassert the Yang's power over the Ying in the same way the Earth occasionally reverses its magnetic polarity; as North becomes South and South becomes North; as tectonic plates realign; as continents shift locations on Earth's surface. He saw Bertie's vision clearly now. She saw herself as a divine change agent. She intended nothing less than to upend the male ordered world of the past six thousand years; and reassert female dominance.

All the world's laws, customs, religious beliefs, and hierarchies had to be scrubbed away and replaced by a new order, which would actually be the old order of six thousand years past, returning to power through Marty and reasserting itself. Bertie would have all the world's women flip a switch in their DNA and emerge from their suffering cocoons to become beautiful seductive butterflies. Men have held the reins of power long enough! It was time for Bertie's great love upheaval that would change all of it. Bertie would mastermind the great change; Marty would be her change agent. Together, they would turn the cultural clock back six thousand years to relive the glorious days of temple prostitution worship.

Bertie intended to launch temple prostitution as a new religion with accompanying rites, music, and evangelizing of nonbelievers to join her new order. She'd rely on the protections offered by the First Amendment to assist her assault on religion and righteousness. Progressive Marxist statists would facilitate Bertie's banishment of God. Bertie would temporarily align her movement with the Marxists. George suddenly visualized the world as Bertie wished it to be. Like an ungulate herd, where the most experienced cow was their leader, people would follow Bertie. Bulls existed only to serve their procreation function; not to rule the herd. In Bertie's new-normal, worldly-ordered human society, people would submissively follow the lead of their most self-confident women. Bertie was on a mission to reinvent God!

"Okay," George saw that Bertie was obsessed with her vision and determined to see it succeed. Nothing would be gained by arguing with her. *"I'll do my part, Bertie. You and Marty can practice her scene shots and position moves with me."* George accepted his role in Bertie's grand plan. It required him to help Marty practice her roles by having frequent sex with her. His eyes assured Bertie he was an enthusiastic volunteer for her cause.

"Good, George; now listen closely to Marty's soft seductive voice while she whispers her next words to her partner:

'I've never been fucked this beautifully, before. It was wonderful! I loved it! I didn't want you to stop, ever!'

"Didn't she voice that line perfectly, George? I want her to build on that sensual tone in her voice. So, while you are practicing with her, I want you to think of things you'd love to hear her saying to you, to bring out your own feelings of love for her; to make you obsess over having intimacy with her. I want the two of you to come up with lines that are very erotic and seductive, got it?"

"Got it, Bertie, I can do that."

"Good, that's my sweetie. Now watch closely, George. Study how her partners' faces look just before they release into her. See how they all adore her? Each of them is smitten. In their faces you can

see how they feel beholden to her for giving them the best sex they've ever had. See how happy she is while they shoot their semen into her mouth?"

"Yes, I see it."

"Good, that's the look I want to see in every scene she does with every partner she has; and I want those partners to look happy, too. So, you'll need to coach the men on that. Can you do that, George?"

"Absolutely, I'll cover that with them before every scene."

"Good, George. Thank you. Now, see how she kisses and sucks the head of each penis AFTER it releases into her mouth, and especially how her tongue stimulates their circumcision circles; and how she continues stroking and sucking more cum from them?"

"Yes, I'm watching. She creates a highly erotic effect by doing that."

"Bingo! Most porn stars stop sucking as soon as ejaculation occurs, but Marty continues romancing the cock. I want that in every fellatio scene she does, George. You'll tell the male partners they are not finished when they come. They'll need to stay with the scene until Marty decides she's finished, got that?"

"Got it. I'll cover that."

"Thank you, George. We're going to create erotic film artistry at its penultimate finest. It will be more breathtaking than fine ballet. Our films will be of a woman enraptured with the perfection of her own artistry. I've never coached anyone who took instructions as well; or who executed as perfectly as Marty. We need to focus on what we have and build on it, George. We have our raw material! This is a fabulous opportunity for all of us. We MUST make the most of it, George. We must help Marty become the very best she can be. We CAN'T let Marty down." Bertie's breath quickened from the excitement of her vision. Her enthusiasm burst through her insistent voice:

"She's spectacular in EVERY WAY, George. If erotica were Olympic competition, I'd score each of Marty's scenes above a perfect

six. Technique, difficulty, rhythm, harmony, flow, grace, creativity, perfection in execution. In EVERY category imaginable in EVERY competition ever devised, Marty scores above perfection. She's the MOST accomplished, MOST glamorous erotic actress the world has ever seen, George. Now, look further along in this film, George, after her four partners have released semen into her. Do you see that huge pool of semen in her vagina?"

"Yes, how could I not see that? It's spellbinding."

"Yes, but it's what she says next that captivates the feelings of the viewers, George. Listen while she whispers to them:

'You men were so wonderful to me. I adore all of you, and I loved feeling the way you made me feel while all of you were shooting your wonderful hot cum into me.'

"Wasn't the way she spoke that line, exquisite? Could you feel the love in her voice? She spoke those words with such incredible sincerity and meaning. I felt she believed and meant every word she said, George. She's not selfish. She never tries to hog all the credit for her beautiful work. She's gracious. She understands she needs great partners to enable her to perform as beautifully as she does. I want that to come through in all her scenes. I want you to think of more lines that she can voice. Will you work on that? Will you go back through her films and think about where she could say more lines? I want her to use her voice much more in her future films, okay?"

"Sure, Bertie, I'll go through them and write more lines for her, then we'll rehearse them with her while we watch her previous films and see if we're giving you what you want, okay?"

"Yes, really good, George; now here's something else that I want to capture. See here, where she's burbling cum on her lips; then taking it into her mouth and smiling? I want her to do more of that. Those film frames capture that divine look on her face. They tell the viewer that her mouth is like a holy altar where life's essences are presented to her through her partners' ejaculations.

"Those frames tell the viewers that she's honored to be the woman into whose mouth her partners repose their life-giving offerings. It's a highly symbolic sequence and it reflects beautifully on how proud she is that they honored her that way. She's extremely proud of her work! There's no trace of shame or embarrassment in her face, only pride and happiness. She's letting the world know she felt honored to be chosen to suck those penises; and she loved doing it.

"There's her joyful smile again! See it? That's her pride showing!" Bertie squealed, *"can you see it in the gleam in her eyes? Did you catch it? Do you see the love? Doesn't she make you feel like holding her and kissing her? She's so lovable and adorable! That's erotica at its finest, George."*

George nodded while keeping his eyes on the screen.

"Her smile inspires confidence. She telegraphs that it's good and wonderful and healthy to seek her and make love with her. Her smile says she expects you to not hold anything back when you make love with her. See her beaming her love so expressively to all of her seven partners? See the love radiating from her face, George?"

"Oh yes, I see what you mean, especially the eyes. She has a beautiful expression."

"Yes, it's breathtaking. It's marvelous. It captivates a viewer and makes him love her. She's not making that up, George. I want you to see where we could work in more of that look."

Bertie's tone dropped an octave as she confided to George:

"I cannot teach that LOOK, George! LOOK at her face, George. Have you ever seen such joy? She LOVED making love with every one of those men. She was thrilled to be doing what she was doing! She was in another world, George. She was so much at home in her element that she didn't want to stop. And then, as the scene was ending, she gave all of them that devilish, coquettish smile of hers; and she licked her lips so sexily. Did you catch the way she folded back the apex of her tongue to expose the frenulum?"

"Yes. What was that about?"

Bertie whispered as if she was in a hushed movie theater:

"That's an extremely aggressive female sexual signal. She's taunting the males, George. She's telling her viewing males she wants them to come to her and pleasure her. She's also making a subconscious communication that she chooses from among many men, takes their semen and does with it as she pleases. She's sending them an unmistakable, unforgettable signal. This film will memorialize her erotic talents through the ages, George. It's classic artistry. It's the raw immorality of her natural uninhibited shamelessness. This is BEFORE we enhance what she does. In that scene she just established herself as the Queen of explicit erotic intimacy.

"Watch now, while I move a few more frames ahead, George. Okay, do you see that? Are you watching this?"

Bertie took her eyes off the screen to see if George was paying attention. She satisfied herself that he was, and returned her gaze to the screen.

"See her lifting that cum from her pool onto her fingers? Now, let's go a little further ahead. There! She's swallowing all that cum from all those handsome young men. She's sending her film partners another subconscious message.

"She's implying that none of them might be the lucky man she chooses to father her baby. She's sending that same subliminal message to the males in her viewing audience. She's letting the entire male world know that she's particular about whom she'll mate with; if she'll even mate with anyone. It's an unspoken, powerful message, George. She's saying she needs time to think about it.

"She's saying she will not surrender her film career and the notoriety that her hard work has accomplished, to become some man's wife. It's her subtle way of challenging the males, daring them to prove to her that they are good enough for her. It's her challenge to

the herd bull of the male organization to come forward and prove himself to her. She's saying she only wants to taste these males' virility for now. That swallowing arouses all male viewers, George. It's her unspoken challenge to them. It makes them want to go to her and prove themselves to her. It makes them want to fight like herd bulls over mating rights. She gave an immensely powerful come-on signal, just then."

"So, she's a tease?"

"Oh yes, George, definitely. She's a beautiful, glorious tease. She's always teasing the males and their penises. But no, she's not a tease in the traditional sense of the word. She doesn't seek to tease so she can let a man down and break his heart. No, quite the opposite, she seeks to tease; draw men in; seduce them; and give every one of them a sensational sexual experience that forever binds their love to her. Watch, George; see what I mean?

"She embraces each male partner, holds his body close and kisses him a soulful French kiss. She appreciates love making, George. She's letting her viewers know she loves having sex with each partner. She's signaling that she's ecumenical. She loves her lovemaking with every man she makes love with. She is not pretending. You're not seeing pretense in any of this. That's what makes her SO beautiful; SO realistic; and SO sexy. She LOVES being a whore. She LOVES lovemaking with those men.

"I LOVE her, George. She's the ALL-MODERN woman. She's LOVELY! She telegraphs her messages subconsciously; letting viewers know that deciding to have a baby and who will father it will be HER decision. Until then, if that time ever even comes, she fully intends to concentrate on her intimate artistry. She makes no bones about it. She loved performing that scene in front of those cameras. That's why she's so special, George." Bertie didn't notice George's nod. She was obsessed with her film study.

PRODUCTION TECHNIQUE

Though this be madness yet there is method in it. (Shakespeare: Hamlet)

"Now Marty, help me understand your director's techniques. When you changed positions for your new partners was that your idea or his?" Bertie, ever the coach, was focused on particular details.

"I was following his instructions when I made those position changes, Bertie," responded Marty. *"He wanted me to love my first partner in the missionary position so he could capture my face."*

"I understand what he was doing. As you were lying down, I loved how your lips invited love making as you smiled. The way you extended your limbs drew every watching heart into your loving embrace. That scene is priceless. Then, in the next scene he has you on top. What was the thinking there?"

"He likes to show me on top. It's his favorite position for filming my body's undulation movements and my face while I make love. He varies his filming from full body, which captures my sinuous rhythms while I slide my vagina over the penis, to close ups of my vagina and mons pubis, while I'm moving rapidly oner it. When I did my Chinese split to make love with my second partner, he wanted to get extreme close ups of my vagina going sliding all the way down over my partner's penis; then showing my lower torso rocking the penis inside me, while grinding my pelvis. He wanted the entire big screen filled with my vagina taking control, sliding down over the penis; then rocking it.

"He captured my face, expressing my delight at how exhilarating that penis felt while it was pulsing inside me; straining to ply my deepest recesses. He also captured my partner's face, expressing his awe over my sexuality. Then he captured my partner's helplessness. He wanted to show, in those close-ups of my partner's face, how it

became impossible for my partner to control his penis's sensations. His face knew that his penis had to surrender to my stimulations. The face showed awe and helplessness. The film captures the sense of my partner's limbic mind; how it recognizes the gloriousness of the moment of ejaculation. The director wanted to show how my partner's willpower vanished, and how his penis released inside me, glorifying my lovemaking. Have you noticed how my partner ejaculated in less than thirty seconds?"

"Yes, I see his cum oozing out of you, washing over his penis. The way that director did that close-up makes the viewers think your vagina is right there in front of their faces. It's graphic and very explicit. It's raw, but extremely powerful. It took my breath away. I liked it. I think we should get several close-up sequences like that in every future film." Bertie made a mental note of the sequence.

'I agree. I liked performing it, too. Very few men can stay inside me when I do that. Watch. When I performed my pitching and yawing pelvic movement with my next partner's penis, he also lost his self-control and quickly shot his semen. His penis slipped out of me while I rocked forward. His semen shot up, and onto my stomach when he lost control. See how his penis spurted its cum like crazy? I thought his face looked boyishly sweet and innocent when that happened."

"Yes. He shot off, just like a typical teenager. I like him. What's his name?" Bertie's eyes stayed riveted to the screen.

"I don't remember."

"That's okay. I'll track him down. I think we could use him again. Any guy who shoots off semen like it's a volcanic eruption makes for great film."

"I agree. I'd love to do him again. He has great vitality. He feels good inside me, too. I only wish he could hold himself back a little longer. My director liked him too. His expression was so natural. I

could see in his face that he loved me. My director decided leave that sequence in the film."

"We're going to use him and have him work with you on the JELLY ROLL move."

"What's that, Bertie?"

"Oh, baby, you're so perfect for it. It's going to be one of your Signature moves in every film. It's the way you smile while you roll your pelvis when you're in Missionary and your vagina is flush with the male's body while his penis is all the way inside you. It's the subtle movements you'll do with your vagina on that penis that give it exactly the right amount of stroke pressure; then you'll release your suction on it, leaving a vacuum hole. Your partner will be unable to resist coming. We'll coordinate your facial expressions with your roll; and we'll pair those with close-ups of your vagina while a soft jazz beat plays in the background. It will captivate the fans. It's the perfect move for you and that young man. Jelly Roll tears the heart out of a man's chest, rips all misogyny from his mind and sucks every drop of cum he has inside him; right out of his scrotum. We'll do it in sync with a perfect musical score. I'll work on it. It will be heavenly. Every man who sees you perform it will agree that intimacy with you is beautiful. He'll appreciate a woman's needs for intimacy like he never did before. And he will love you forever. The image of you doing that move will stay in his mind, forever."

"Kind of like I'm riding a horse, and loving my horse, is that it?"

"Yes, sort of. George and I will show you. We do it often. Okay, now let's go on. What am I seeing here?"

"This third man had just mounted me doggie style. My director wanted to show my vagina from the PB, or 'Pussy from Behind' view. He wanted me to take my partner's penis all the way inside me; then he wanted extreme close ups of my vagina while I rapid twerked.

"Whenever I rapid twerk with a penis inside me I immediately get super-hot and super slippery. Most partners can't resist that

sensation. They quickly lose control. That third partner also shot off in less than thirty seconds. See that?"

"Yes. He didn't last long, either."

"No, he didn't. None of them do." Marty's voice was frustrated. *"It's me. I can't help myself. It's how I get when I do PB. Having a penis inside me, that way, gets me crazy excited; and I twerk too fast. That's what feels best for me, but I make the penises shoot too quickly. My directors typically like to film me making love for between a half hour and a full hour, before the male partner ejaculates; so, when I make my partners come quickly like that, the filming must stop, until my partner gets himself hard again. But some directors know me very well. They know I get crazy when I twerk like that, so they anticipate me and have extra, already hardened, penises standing by, ready for me.*

"Time delays and spare penises run up directors' costs, so I try to be mindful of what I'm doing on set. Understand that I love to just let myself go and fuck like crazy, especially when I'm twerking; but often that's not what the director wants. Notice how semen from the first and second partners was already flowing out of me before I even started doing my third partner? Some fans don't like to see that, but others can't get enough of it. This director wanted to leave that flowing cum in the film. What did you think, Bertie?"

"I think it needs to come out." Bertie shook her head slowly, thoughtfully. *"While some fans might love the carnal nature of it, it detracts from your high-class image. You want every viewer fantasizing that he's your only partner. Lots of men dream they're your only lover. Having other men's semen oozing from you detracts from that image. You can't have both a high-end image and a barnyard image.*

"We must choose our market. The money is in the high-end market and your Premium Members Service. Let's take that scene out of there. Kill it. Tell that director if he wants to show you as

a street slut again, you won't work with him. We will enforce the brand image WE want."

"But Bertie, I love to wet fuck. It gives me my slutty, naughty girl feeling; and I love that feeling!"

"Listen. I'm the coach. I'm the brains that will put you on top. I say it goes out. It's out."

"Okay, Bertie. I'll do as you say," agreed a reluctant Marty, *"tell me what you think of this last bit of film. I was doing a back bridge, head upside down sucking my first partner's penis, while I held my legs open so my second partner's penis could get great penetration of my vagina, while he stood over me. He held me up by my tush so he could get totally inside me.*

"I loved how I felt, because his rock-hard penis was rubbing firmly against my clit. The blood rushing to my head gave me a euphoric sensation. I felt like I was just short of blacking out. I was coming with a steady, gushing orgasm while sucking my second partner. It was easy to control the flow of my orgasm. His penis gave me just the right touch of clit stroking; and he kept me flowing. I felt beautiful, like it wouldn't ever end, until I wanted it to end. It was totally mind blowing. The director captured my feelings perfectly. I love being fucked that way. I don't get to do it very often. I think we should try working more contortion scenes into my films. What do you think?"

"I'd like to think about it." Bertie brought her finger to the side of her cheek. *"We're trying to brand you as a sex goddess, not some contortionist for a Las Vegas floor show. Even though you love having sex that way I think it hurts your brand image. We're aiming to lock in a very high-class image for you with your film art. We want viewers to pay premium prices to buy your films. We are going to change the way people view adult film artistry. We'll create premium content, high brow erotica that's acknowledged and embraced as Avant Garde artistry in polite sophisticated circles."*

"And contortion art doesn't fit?" Marty voiced chagrin. *"You can't work some contortion positions into some scenes for me? I love performing that way. I love stretching myself out; my body arched over the floor while my head is upside down and my mouth is performing fellatio; and while my other partner performs cunnilingus or simply holds me by my pelvis while he fucks me. It feels so marvelously different. It's very exciting, Bertie. It breaks up the monotony of always fucking in the standard, strait-laced positions. Please."*

"It doesn't fit the image I want. Not really. Some who watch adult films like watching a woman ravaged like a piece of meat at some sex-fest, free-for-all fraternity party. Some want to see a freak show. But the others are the people who have the money. They like what I'd call soft, hard-core intimacy. That implies romance. They want to see a woman enjoying the act of love making and loving the man or men who make love with her. We are going to expand that market by providing premium content for that last group, which also happens to include married women. You're going to be the most seductive, most appealing, classiest love making woman who has ever appeared on screen.

"Every one of your scenes will feature you performing beautiful erotic love making, filled with believable romantic scenarios, brimming with credible dialog themes and lines; and all your partners will understand that they are on set with you to LOVE you and to MAKE LOVE with you; VERY SWEET, GENUINE, BELIEVABLE LOVE with you. They are NOT going on set with you to fuck you senseless, bang your brains out, or to prove you know how to fuck while your body is doing weird, twisted contortions. There's a HUGE difference. We will differentiate your art by making you a compelling, believable love object; and we'll showcase that difference.

"You will not perform any pig in the barnyard scenes; nothing that disgusts or weird's people out; no contortions, none; no scenes where you are abused in any way whatsoever. From now on, you are a divine goddess. You are a cut above all the women who do those other things. Even though you like the kinky fun of it, you are not going to be doing that stuff on film. Got it?"

"Yes, Mother, that I didn't have. I've got it." Marty voiced her dejected disappointment."

"Good girl. From now on I want you always thinking of yourself as Marty, Love Goddess. When you perform, I want you thinking that you are gracing the great unwashed with your magnificent, glorious love making. You will show viewers how to entice, seduce, and be loving lovers. They will see how enjoyable and beautiful love making can and should be; and how a woman should feel like she's a heaven-sent goddess while she's making love, understand?"

"Yes Bertie."

"Very good, Marty. Now, listen to my thought. We're going to take your natural enthusiasm and package it in a way that exemplifies incomparable excellence. I've observed you and your feelings as you expressed them in your films. We're going to enhance what comes natural for you, okay?"

"For example?"

"Okay, the first change we are going to make will be with your facial ejaculation scenes. You are no longer going to kneel patiently before your partners, with your mouth open and your tongue extended outward while they whack themselves off. That's the image of a servant girl. It's not what we want. It stops."

"But what should I do?"

"You take charge, that's what. You are the Goddess of Intimacy. You do not wait for your partner to bless you with a cum

shot. Instead, you grasp his testicles with one hand and massage his balls. And with your other hand, you grasp the shaft of his penis. And here's the key to showcasing your insatiable craving for semen. Your shaft hand rapidly, furiously, strokes his penis; far faster that he would stroke it. Your mindset will be that you are demanding that penis surrender up its semen to you. You take control of that penis. You let your viewers know that your partner's penis belongs to you; not to him. Once a man has fornicated with your vagina or your mouth, he gives up all control of his penis to you, from that moment on. You show the cameras how craven you are; how you demand that that penis surrender its semen to you."

"And I still shoot it into my mouth, right?"

"Yes, of course. And you will feel the penis is ready to release to you by the pressure you feel in your stroking fingers. The release will not be some uncontrolled eruption all over your lovely face and chin. You will hold the penis head over your extended tongue, and place its head slightly into your opened mouth. I want the close-up cameras to capture the semen eruption flow leaving the penis head and going into your mouth. You are the star of the scene, not the penis. Remember that. Got it?"

"Yes, Bertie. Got it. I can do it that way; and I think I'll like that much better."

"Good girl. And there's another change I'd like to make. When a penis begins ejaculating inside your vagina, the instant that it starts coming, I want you to grab it with your hand and pull it our of you. I want it to shoot some semen onto your outer vaginal lips and onto your mons pubis. I want your fans to see that the penis is in the process of ejaculating. Then, after it spurts some visible semen onto your vagina, I want you to grab the penis with both your hands and reinsert it into your vagina; and I want you to take it all the way in, all the way in to the bottom of its shaft. And I want you to wrap your *arms around your partner and kiss him fully on the mouth; and I want you to then say:*

'I love what you're doing to me right now. I love how your warm cum feels on my clitoris.'

"*And then, I want you to prolong your capture of the penis while you French kiss your partner and moan about how wonderful this feels and how you want him to do this with you more often. Can you do that?*"

"*Yes, and with pleasure. I love where you're going with this, Bertie.*"

"*It's branding, sweetheart. We'll be branding you as the undisputed Goddess of erotic romance. Now, here's another change we'll make. When your partners have entered you from behind, doggie style, I want to communicate to the viewers that they have surrendered control of their penises to the world's most insatiable, erotically romantic woman who has ever performed before a camera. I want you to twerk on that penis like you've become a demon possessed; and I want you to gyrate wildly on it. I want that viewer to gasp in fear of the penis staying attached to your partner. I want to see you go wild on it and make it come as quickly as possible. Can you do that?*"

"*Yes, of course I can. I love to twerk and bounce and grind like that. It's very natural for me. But that partner will come very quickly; and my producers and directors don't like that.*"

"*Well, that's not going to be their call. That's our call. I'm your agent. If they want slow motion, they don't get Marty. If they want a lot of camera time for the doggie style look, they'll need to come up with some scenes that have you twerking more than one penis. How many should I tell them you could do in a half hour shooting?*"

"*Oh, at least one every two minutes; so, tell them I'd do fifteen, easily.*"

"Okay, very good. Now I have one more thing I want to do. This will establish you as the undisputed Queen of Intimacy. We'll do some thematic films. George and I will produce them. I know what I want. Our first one will be a Fourth of July theme. We'll be honoring the incredible freedoms that America bestows upon its citizens. You will dress in a string bikini with American flag red, white and blue, with white stars material. You will be at poolside, in a lounge chair.

"There will be some twenty men and twenty women milling around, sipping their drinks. A man will come up to you and take you by the hand. You'll giggle and ask him what he's doing. He'll tell you he wants to honor America's birthday and its wonderful freedoms. He'll walk you over to where there's a rubber mat by the pool. The Star-Spangled Banner will begin playing. You will solemnly place your hand over your heart and mouth the Anthem's words, showing how much you appreciate and honor our wonderful country, which allows you to freely perform your explicit erotica romance scenes. Then, after the Anthem, patriotic music from John Phillip Sousa's marches will begin playing very, very softly, as background music. Your partner will hold you in his arms and begin kissing you. You will reciprocate. You will French kiss him while he fondles your breasts and kisses your neck and fingers your vagina. You will giggle with pleasure while he undoes your bikini top and pinches and kisses your nipples. What I want you to communicate to the viewers is that explicit erotica is very much the American Way; that it is very patriotic; very expressive of our wonderful freedoms. Got it?"

"Yes." I love the theme, Bertie.

"Good. Next, you will feel for his penis while he undoes your bikini bottom and rubs your mons pubis. Other men will join the two of you on the mat. They will bring huge pool pillows for you to recline on. Once you retrieve his penis from his swimming trunks, you will begin performing fellatio on it. Meanwhile, other men will come to you and

lift you to your feet. No fewer than twenty men will then take turns holding you close to them and kissing you. You will respond by caressing their necks and French kissing all twenty of them.

"While the patriotic music plays, they will all grope you and kiss your breasts and neck, and shoulders, and ass; basically, the will kiss you everywhere on your body. You will smile broadly and giggle joyously; and squeak at your pleasures of being fondled. Remember, we are convincing the world that we are thrilled with America's blessings that allow us to create explicit adult content. And we love bringing our joy to the world. Your partners will then lift you onto the pillow arrangement. You will smile, spread your legs widely, and moan with pleasures as you will then receive cunnilingus from several of them.

"Many women will join in a festive, patriotic expression of freedom by also performing cunnilingus with you. You will have maiden position sex with all twenty of the men; and perform fellatio with each of them. But each partner will have plenty of time with you. Your fellatios will include loving, adoring, joyfully pleasing, lickings of the entire shaft of every penis. I want your most sincere feelings of love and intimacy communicated with every single partner. None of this will be hurried. We can take breaks in the filming. You'll get all the rest you need.

"You will also perform some scenes with multiple partners, where you are enjoying fornication at the same time you are performing fellatio and some cunnilingus with your female partners. But we will only give very small, necessary, roles to the other females. We will be ninety-five percent filming you and your mouth and vagina. We will patiently capture all the eroticism you can possible express with every partner in every scene. I want you to feel genuine love for every one of your partners. Always, always, remember to smile. You love sex; and I want you to constantly communicate that. It will take

time, but it will be worth it. We will stop shooting frequently to lube you and rest you. This may take several days. I want you to have cameo intercourse sessions with every individual partner."

"But Bertie, several days, twenty men and twenty women. The agency costs will go overtime. It could cost you a fortune, easily over a hundred thousand."

"I don't care what it costs," smiled Bertie smugly. "Do we care what it costs, George?"

"We don't care what it costs," replied always agreeable George.

Bertie continued: "I will produce a continuous, poolside orgy, patriotic themed film. But at the end, I will edit into the film individual cameos of each partner holding you, touching you, fingering you, kissing you, performing cunnilingus and fellatio and fornication with you; kind of like credits in a regular film, understand?"

"Yes, Bertie, understood. You are a genius."

"Thank you. And for the ending sequence of the film, we will use sound track from the serenity theme of the Richard Russel, Robert Russel Bennet production of Victory at sea. It's very sweet and soothing. It communicates that all is right and good with the world. While this music plays, you will, casually, lovingly, and respectfully, take one penis after another into your hands and unhurriedly, adoringly, kiss it and suck it, all done in a very erotic, intimate way. What we will be communicating to our viewers is that we are very grateful for the many who have sacrificed and died to give us the freedom to create our exquisite intimacy artistry. We are expressing, through erotic romantic scenes and music, our profound and deep love of America. Got it?"

"Yes, got it. And loving it! Loving all of it! I can't wait to perform it. Thank you, Bertie."

"Yes, 'got it' is the right answer and the right attitude. Good girl. I'll also be working up a film score for Christmas where we will softly play songs like 'Silent Night,' 'Away in a Manger,' 'Joy to the world,'

and several others; all played as soft, background music. Our goal will be to communicate how much we appreciate America's religious freedoms and religious tolerances, even as adult film makers. You will help people see that love making is not just a bodily function; but rather a beautiful, celebratory, interpersonal experience. You'll show them the range of that experience is from the delicate to the intense; and you'll help them understand how to enjoy every manifestation of love making. You will smile, laugh out loud, giggle and banter seductively with your partners because you will be showing the world how much you love making love; how beautiful and enjoyable it is; and you will be begging your partners to release their semen inside you, because that helps you cherish your shared intimacy.

"Let's ask George this question: *George, darling, what, from a man's viewpoint, is the most important feature of every porn film?*" Both women looked to George for his answer.

He thought a while before he spoke. Then: "*Well, I look to see a woman with a beautiful face. In Marty's face, I see stunning, unforgettable beauty. And I see something much more. I see a woman who feels no trace of guilt or inhibition about performing in her films. I see complete innocence in her immoral fellatios and fornications; as if they are completely natural and without any guilt associated with them in any way; as if creating intimate artistry was her God given mandate to perform without any inhibition or shame or guilt of any sort whatsoever. I see in her face the message that what she is doing is glorious and beautiful; even righteous. And, the main thing, for me at least, is having the feeling that the woman is enjoying herself.*

"*I must see that she loves what she is doing; that she loves fucking and sucking the male penis. That's what makes it or breaks it for me. If the woman is smiling and giggling, and giving every possible signal that she's enjoying the sex, having the time of her life, and loving her experience, then I'm happy for her. I feel a surge in my own penis as blood rushes into it and I imagine that I am the one on screen who is so fortunate to be her lover. I guess it's the mental limbic thing. When a woman creates that feeling in me, I know she is an artist. I feel good for her and for what she's doing; and, in a vicarious way, I fall in love with her. And Marty does create all these erotic feelings inside me."*

George and Marty looked into each other's eyes and smiled a knowing smile to each other. They knew they were blessed to soon become lovers. It was only a matter of time.

"Well, see Marty?" remarked Bertie. *"There it is. If I understand what it takes to wow an audience; and if we execute well, I have no doubt that you will be established as the ultimate Queen of all Intimacy Artistry; the Goddess of all erotic romance; and the most beloved actress in the world; not just of erotica films; but of everything; above all other actresses. And I also forecast that your films and your income will exceed the downloads and incomes of the next five hundred porn stars, combined. Marty, my sweet baby, we will suck all the oxygen and all the money out of the room. When we release our films, the demand for all other erotic actresses will collapse. We will smother and suffocate all your competition. Leave it to Bertie.*

"You'll be showing people the feelings they can achieve during love making. You're now, no longer a bump and grind porn star. You're someone special now. You have special gifts. You have the world's most beautiful face and body; and you've been blessed with the most sex appeal of any woman in the world. You are the world's best explicit film artisan. You specialize in performing the world's most breathtakingly beautiful, erotic, romantic love scenes, okay?"

"Yes Bertie. I'm okay with it."

"Good. Always hold onto those thoughts. When you feel you must have a kinky experience or a wet fuck fest, you can always do that off screen, Okay?"

"Yes, Bertie. I said yes. Okay?" Marty's voice betrayed a touch of annoyance.

"Yes, okay. Look, you'll see. The rewards will be well worth it. Now, what are we looking at next?"

"Okay Bertie, well after I came out of my back bridge contortion, I went into a sitting position to suck both of those partners. I could see that my sucking was getting my final two partners very excited. They could barely contain themselves. They said they'd never seen a chick suck so beautifully before; then they begged me to hurry and finish. They were about to spurt their cum, from just watching me.

"After I finished sucking, my director wanted me back in my missionary position. He wanted to film the awestruck look on my next two partners' faces when they saw my butterfly tattoo. He tilted my pelvis high up on a pillow, so I'd hold their semen inside me during our final scene. That's where I showed my vagina's semen pool, before lifting it into my mouth.

"But see, Bertie, at the very end of the film, how I stood and held each partner close to me and French kissed them? That finishing touch was my idea. I insisted those intimate kissing's stay in the film, uncut. I wanted each lover to know that I loved him as a human being. Each of them left that set feeling the sweetness of our love making. I want to give that erotic romance feeling to my partners. I want them to remember they partnered with me; and experienced intimate wonders with me. I want them to say they lived in the time of Marty. Did you like that final touch?"

"Yes, I did, I loved it! Thank you, Marty," said Bertie, *"that's a wonderful feeling about your partners. That's the feeling I ALWAYS want. Watching your warmth, humanity and love warmed my heart. We'll keep that tenderness and those embraces in all your future work. Now, let's look at some frames from this next film. Something was happening to you before you even started kissing that first man. What was his name?"*

LOVER JOSH

In her first passion, woman loves her lover, in all others all she loves is love. (Lord Byron: Don Juan)

"His name is Josh, why?"

"Look closely, frame by frame. Do you see it? Your skin was turning red. What were you feeling?"

"Oh, hee, hee," Marty giggled like an embarrassed schoolgirl.

"That's the Josh effect. Josh always makes that happen for me. It's my urge to make love with him. It magically arises in the depths of my loins. An electric charge starts sizzling in my sex. My vagina starts acting up, like it's a joyful little puppy, thrilled to see him. I must get closer to him. I'm drawn toward him by an invisible magnetic force. I want to be with him, wiggle my body like crazy inside his arms, and feel his touches all over me; and get shivers of anticipation from his kisses on my cheeks and neck, before he even starts kissing my lips. I start salivating, thinking about the joys I'll feel while he makes love with me.

"I'm anxious for my director to say 'action.' I'm already turned on just by being in Josh's presence." Marty's excitement over Josh was palpable. *"I know we'll be performing several minutes of fore-play for the cameras. I know I'll love the ways he'll touch me; so lovingly; so sensitively. I'm so anxious to make love with him I know I could begin without foreplay. I begin craving every look and touch he's going to give me. Those feelings happen whenever I know Josh will be my partner. Seeing Josh, knowing I'll be on set with him, even makes my fingers feel like they're already wrapped around his amazingly hard penis. I imagine holding it, kissing its head, and guiding it into my vaginal lips, before I even touch it. I imagine his penis touching and probing my outer lips; seeking permission; persuading*

me to spread my legs; eager to enter my slippery heat, before he even stands next to me and takes me in his arms.

"My tongue imagines Josh's tongue playing love dances with it before he even kisses my lips. My body quivers. I melt. We'll soon be like two violins playing beautiful music in perfect harmony. My thoughts hum soft music in my mind. I imagine powerful sensations rushing through my entire body when I thrust against Josh's marvelous penis, even before he embraces me. These sensations flood my feelings before Josh even stands beside me.

"I love the way he stimulates me with his fingers and the heel of his palm. I responsively lift my pelvis to his wonderful, educated hand. I become desperate to begin. My mind does summersaults, imagining that I'm already kissing the tip of his beautiful spear. It is rock hard, like a rod of steel. It's dying to enter me and be inside me. I wait breathlessly, imagining he's already beginning to impale me. I love every second of those anticipation moments.

"I let Josh know I want more. My body tells him he has reached my deepest feelings; and, he's opened me to receive love. My moans urge him to take me to that mystical place where my emotions surrender to him in endless bursts of passion. I want to cross over that mysterious boundary where my passions blur into love; where I just hold on tightly to this magnificent man; and I no longer know the difference between those two emotional pulls; nor do I care. I just want Josh. I want to be with him. I want all of him.

"Josh and I couple our feelings together, during our magical foreplay, before he even nudges my legs and opens my thighs. He tenderly nibble-bites my nipples. He tugs on my buttons, gently, with his lips. Those loving lip tugs confirm that he knows me. He understands my urges have ignited my passion. It's his silent way of letting me know that he understands me. He knows how badly I need him. He knows I am slippery wet and hot inside. He's telling

me I won't have to wait much longer. He will soon enter me. I love when he kisses my buds like that. I adore him. He is my god. His magnificent penis will soon bless me. There's a holy aspect to our love making. It's that special.

"I imagine that my nipple buds become the tongues of asps. They return Josh's nipple pulls. They are my love venom. They draw his soul away from every other lover he has ever known. They captivate Josh's soul and take it away from all his other women and give it to me. His captured soul plunges down into this deep abyss where my soul dwells. There it binds with my soul for all eternity. Our souls wrap their arms and legs around each other. His soul lives there, in eternity with my soul, in our shameless never-ending world of sins and pleasures.

"I soon raise my breasts to meet Josh's nipple tugs. That tells him I am unapologetic. It assures him that I will enjoy my wanton shamelessness. I let him know I want my soul to devour his soul; and I'll never relax my immoral hold on it. My kisses tell him my passion abyss is eternal. The way I press my body to his tells him l will hold his soul there, with mine; inside mine, forever.

"My feelings reach a dizzying intensity. They overwhelm me. They go far beyond the feelings I have for my other film partners. They tell me I must have Josh all to myself, forever. I can not allow any other woman to have him. I can't understand or explain my fevered intensity. I only know it's real. I understand that Josh is pop-ular on the erotic film circuit. Other women love to make love with him. But my feelings persist, after we make love. They stay with me and never leave me.

"I've asked myself if I've gone insane over Josh. I have the same feelings for him as I have with Bob. But Josh is out of reach, somehow. Unlike Bob, I never know when I'll see Josh. That makes him more enticing, somehow. I ask myself: 'Can I love two men with intensity that goes beyond making love for a film; and beyond the love I feel

for my Premium Members?' I cannot answer my own question, nor can my voices help me. It's a depth of feeling I can't explain.

"As the moment approaches for Josh to enter me, I become indescribably steamy and slippery hot. I tell him I want him. I know he's there, ready to come inside me. I've touched him, stroked him. He's so hard, so strong. I welcome him into my temple of endless pleasure paths. My vagina transforms. My welcoming love maker becomes this wild, insatiable, shamelessly independent organ. It wants to hold Josh's penis inside it forever. My feelings turn possessive. I cling. I dig my nails into Josh's back. My skin heats up. I am on fire. I want to fuck and never stop.

"Bertie, when I open my arms to embrace Josh, I'm already thinking these thoughts. That's why my blood rushes into my skin. I get that way around Josh. We make love fantastically well together. I love making love with him."

"But Marty, you just made love with two other men, before you ever even started kissing Josh. How could you feel a heat flush after that? What was happening to your body? What made you so hot for Josh?"

"I can't explain it, Bertie, it happens. It's his amazing cock. It's my nymphomania. When it switches on, I have this flash. It starts deep inside my brain. I notice it there, first; like some dam has burst; and hot liquid has erupted inside my head. Then that flash feeling rushes like a surging flood into the front of my brain. It shuts out all my other thoughts; and it takes complete control of my mind. It tells me I must have Josh. It's a madness. At this point I would kill to have him. The intensity of my feelings is that strong. I need to make love with him, right there; right away; unscripted.

"My vagina gets this 'I must have him' urge. It displaces all my other feelings. This urge feeling compels and dominates my behavior from that moment onward. It's overwhelming. It's an uncontrollable, deep churning, restless heat that cries out to take Josh completely

inside of me. I let my entire being explode all around his delicious, wonderful penis. My vagina can't wait to surround it, hold it inside, and gush all over it. Explicit images flash through my mind. My mind is morning sunshine. It blinds my sight. I can't see anything other than Josh's gorgeous penis. My mind speaks to my opening rose bud; shakes her awake to the wonder of life and the magnificence of sex. It tells her "Wake up sleepy head! Open! Display your petals so butterfly Josh will thrust his proboscis into you. I'm helpless when I feel all this emotion, Bertie. I can't resist it. I can't explain it. I just know I must satisfy it."

"I'm fascinated by the way you turned on when you approached Josh. You started licking his neck and his ear and moving your body closer and closer to his." Bertie's eyes questioned Marty, trying to understand the younger woman's body chemistry. *"Then, when he responded by putting his arm around you, you began seductively rubbing your hand over his penis. I sensed you were letting him know that you had to have it; that you were trying to be very patient while you made him hard, before you opened his pants and peeled them down. And, then you continued kissing his neck, right where his Adam's apple is; before you French kissed his mouth. As a viewer I couldn't wait until you pulled his pants down and took his penis into your mouth. And then, the way you licked it, from the base of its scrotum to the tip of its head; that slow, beautifully seductive manner you repeatedly performed, made me feel Josh's feelings. He had to know he was experiencing the most erotic fellatio any man has ever known.*

"And then I was drawn to how you kissed his penis's head and massaged it with your tongue; so lovingly, and so patiently. That was such explicit, mouthwatering erotica it made me feel like I was there in the film, licking Josh's penis, myself. I even imagined I was sharing it with you. And, after it became so incredibly hard, I was awed by how you straddled it while Josh sat in that chair. You first mounted

it with your back to Josh's face. Your vagina was visibly hot and wet, do you remember how you felt?"

"Yes, Bertie, I remember. I always remember when Josh's penis first enters me. I tremble. It's a divine feeling; a holiness. I feel like I'm finally where I want to be for the rest of my entire life. I want to cherish that feeling; hold onto it; appreciate the majesty of it; never let it go."

Bertie sighed a dreamy sigh. *"It was so beautifully done, Marty. I was fascinated by the cameras' close up shots of that entry. You did this after you did your first two partners, right?"*

"Yes. After."

"You glistened. Your vaginal lips were morning dew on a rip-ened, freshly opened peach. Your juices visibly gleamed on your outer lips. Did you lube for that?"

"No, Bertie. I didn't have to. Not for Josh. I'm so turned on by him, I never have to lube for Josh. Just being near him gets me that hot and slippery. Did you like the entry scene close-up?"

"Yes, it was spectacular. I mean I could feel how much you loved having his penis entering you, by the way you smiled and rolled your eyes back; and how you moved your head from side to side. I mean, I could feel it happening as if it was happening to me. You were experiencing something euphoric, weren't you?"

"Oh yes, I was. Absolutely, I was. I knew I had the penis of the one man I truly love deeply inside me. There's a suddenness that happens with my body when Josh first penetrates me. It's like my vagina and my whole body tries to tell him that I love him more than anything else in the world; and I want him to say with me, forever. I knew we were going to make beautiful love that day; and I was so grateful for that. My body was trying to express that, too. It was already antici-pating having many lovely orgasms. I always feel like that with Josh."

Bertie looked in awe at her young star. *"He's that meaningful to you, isn't he?"*

"Yes. Definitely, he is. My body doesn't lie to me."

"I could feel that, too. It's a need you have. I saw it growing when he put his hands on your stomach, and you laid your head back on his shoulder; and the two of you kissed while you began to come, I began masturbating. I believed then, and I do now, that the two of you were making the most beautiful pornographic scene ever filmed. It was spectacular. It was more than erotica. It was unbounded love. Your need was growing, wasn't it?"

"Oh yes. And it would keep on growing, right through my orgasm and afterwards."

"I know how you felt, dear child. I was living it with you. While I watched that scene, I felt myself falling in love with you. I knew I wanted you. I've never seen a more breathtaking seduction. It was beyond beautiful; beyond erotic. Empathy. That's what you brought out of me: empathy. And this was all happening before you performed your most explicit love making. My mouth watered as he massaged your vagina with his hand while he thrusted into you. Your pelvis was rocking back and forth over his penis, and your eyes became glazed. Your orgasm began then, didn't it?"

"Yes, that's when the flood started."

"I noticed how you began moving faster and faster; and he was all the way in, then. Didn't that hurt you, a little?"

"No, not at all. I love the pressure feeling. It doesn't hurt me. It stimulates me to thrust harder. I love it when we both get intense like that."

"And then, you continued flowing like a river. I watched your face while you kissed him. You were smiling. And at the same time, you were wincing with the intensity of your flow, weren't you?"

"Yes, but understand; the wince wasn't from pain. I was loving his thrusts and rocking with them. The wince was me feeling my inner ecstasy, Bertie. It's like that when I make love with Josh. I can't help myself. I only know I need to let myself go; completely feel the moment."

"I could tell you were having huge feelings. I felt them too. I was feeling them with you. Watching you flowing like that gave me this huge burst of warmth in my breast. My heart began pounding with lust for you. I felt adoration and glowing love. It was like a wave swept over me. It was surreal. I felt your other-worldly serenity, all through those moments. Later, when Josh lifted you up and stood you on one foot, his arm under your other leg, supporting you, while he thrusted into you, I noticed the way you looked into his eyes; and how you smiled to him. You were flowing a river of emotion while he held you that way, weren't you?"

"Yes, I was. I can't stop it once it starts. My emotions come into sync with my orgasm flow. I have to let them run their course. While I'm having a prolonged orgasm with Josh, like that one, I must let it continue. I can't let any other thoughts intrude on my happiness. I'm a total woman then. My eyes express that I've lost all sense of myself. My feelings become heaven. I'm just pouring out love then. All is wonderful. My euphoria must never end."

"I felt it right along with you, baby. You did so much more than make beautiful film. You expressed intimate, erotic love. You captured the honest shameless beauty of it. You had no inhibitions whatsoever. You also captured Josh's feelings. He became emotionally entwined with you. He was spellbound. His feelings were inside your beautiful orgasm. He adores you. I saw that by the way he looked at you. He appreciated your feelings. It was incredibly beautiful. You honestly love this man, don't you, baby?"

Marty thought: *'It's totally weird the way she keeps calling me baby, like I'm her daughter, or something. She is a bit off; and a whole lot bossy. But they are paying me my Premium Member rates; giving me free run of their mansion; and spending all this time and effort to make me into a top performing porn star. I can't complain. It's their money. They want to play house, I'll play along. They want to live in mental fantasy land. I won't stop them.'*

"Yes," Marty replied to Bertie, *"a thousand times yes, Bertie. I am madly in love with him. I love watching his face while he makes love with me. I know he feels the same love for me that I feel for him. I could love him like that in thousands of scenes; forever."*

"I saw that love, Marty. I fell deeply in love with you while I watched. And then, toward the end of that scene, when you took his penis into your mouth and performed fellatio again, I saw your face light up with joy when he came inside your mouth. I watched awestruck while you continued sucking his penis; and licking semen from it; and finally swallowing it. Do you remember what you said then?"

"Yes, Bertie, I said: "You are fantastic. I loved every minute. I loved how you made me feel. I love you. I want you to know: I really, honestly, love you."

"Yes, those were your exact words. They were convincing because you really felt that way. When I heard you speak those words, I fell in love with your honest innocence. Even though you have other lovers; and they could see your film with Josh, and hear what you said to him, that didn't make you pause. You told Josh how you felt. You were completely honest when you told Josh you loved him. I felt it.

"When I saw that film, and heard you speak those words to Josh, I wanted you. I dream about that scene. Whenever I think of it, I want to take you in my arms and love you; love you for being such a glorious, open, unapologetic adorable woman. The scene endears me to you, to your casual, honest immorality. It makes me want to kiss you to pleasure you, as my humble way of honoring what you do; the emotions you create within me; and I want to kiss your mouth to be closer to your innermost feelings; and I want to hug you tightly to let you know how deeply I care about you. It's all beautiful; and it feels so right to love you like I do."

"Thank you, Bertie, I appreciate your feelings. I want to feel them in my mouth. I want you, too. And I want to make love with you, too. We'll be beautiful together."

"I know we will. I feel it. Let's try to work some more. Tell me more about Josh. How did you two become so personally attached?"

"Sure, Bertie, I already knew Josh very well. We had performed together about seven times before this film. I knew how he touches; how he makes love; and I loved all of it. I just loved being with him. I had become very familiar with his fabulous penis and how beautifully it performs inside me. When I'm on top facing him, I collapse my body onto his, and French kiss him while I twerk. He has perfected this masterful technique where he holds me close with his arm over the small of my back; and while he uses the fingers of his other hand to stimulate my crown area while he thrusts, as I twerk. The effect is nirvana on steroids. My mind simply lifts up and away from the world into this holy place where everything is possible, and everything is wonderful; and everyone is accepting the glory of my immorality.

"He makes me feel so good about myself and my promiscuity. Then, when he's ready, he lifts his eyebrows and face ever so slightly, twice. That's my signal. He's silently asking me if I want him to release his cum inside me and whether I'm ready for it. I think he does that out of love. He wants me to have time to position my clitoris against the opening of his penis, so I'll feel the full gush and the heat of his release. He knows that release will intensify my orgasm and send me my rapture pleasures. When I have my vagina positioned exactly right, I nod my 'yes' to him; and then I just press tightly to him and hang on. My insides glow while he comes inside me. He always spurts his hot lava flows directly against my clitoris. It's the release of conception's lust forces. It's what causes new creation. I can sense that creation happening. It's fulfilling; so meaningful. It's consummation of love, and it's beautiful.

"I love Josh's penis. I sometimes dream about it, even when I'm with Bob. I often dream I'm playing with it; romancing it, licking, and sucking it, guiding it into my vagina and feeling it stroking over my clitoris; and then thrusting my pelvis against it, feeling it hard against my clit; sending tremors of feelings through my clitoral nerves, making me orgasm like I'm a crazed wild animal. Those dreams are so wonderful."

"Marty let's rerun those last few frames. You're kissing Josh and telling him you love him. But I noticed that your voice was breaking up, and you have tears in your eyes. What caused that emotion?"

"Oh, Bertie, you would catch that. I was dying inside. Josh told me he was going away for a year. He wanted to travel the world; work at becoming an artist; and just ski and surf all over the world. He told me he wanted to catch the thrills. You know, the best snowy powder; the biggest ocean waves. He's an expert skier and surfer. I was holding him in my arms for what I knew might be our last time for a long time; possibly forever. I was breaking up inside because I love him so much. I realized that I might never make love with him again. It was a horrible feeling.

"He had asked me to run away with him, but I didn't want to leave Bob. I was holding him in my arms, desperately trying to hold on to those final moments; hoping they'd last a little longer. I haven't seen him for two months now. I'm hoping he'll come back to me. I desperately want to make more films with him. I feel empty without him. I need him in my life."

"But why didn't you go with him? He's a beautiful man."

"Yes, he's Adonis. He's the most beautiful man with the most gorgeous body and splendid penis I've ever made love with. But, Bertie, you'd have to know Bob. He's also a beautiful man. And, Bertie, Bob loves me, only me. Josh isn't a one-woman man like Bob is. I

need Bob more than I could ever need Josh. I don't expect you to understand everything that goes on in my mind, Bertie; but I love both men. I began crying because I knew Josh was leaving me; and I didn't know when I could make love with him again. I need to make love with Josh, Bertie. He completes me in a way no other man does. Can you understand that?"

"Of course, I can, dear. I'm sure Josh loves you deeply, too. He won't stay away long. I'm sure he'll come back to you. What I saw of the two of you was something special. I'm sure he'll get in touch. You'll see. If he doesn't call you soon, I'll find him and persuade him to return to you. You will have Josh in your future films. Bertie will make sure of it. I can be persuasive. And I have a great deal of money. I want him on call for all your films. I want you to be happy, baby. If you want to make love with Josh, you will have him."

"Oh, Bertie, thank you. I hope you're right. I really need him. He's the one performer that totally completes me when he releases inside me. All the strength and wonder of that perfectly muscled, beautiful man suddenly relaxes and it lets go of his splendid life forces; and then it's all flowing naturally, lovingly from him into me. He holds me tightly while this release happens. I feel I'm in the arms of this human Adonis. I surrender myself. I am powerless. I must let him have me, all of me, for as long as he wants me. I feel his need for me. And I want to always be there to fill it. It's so beautiful. Each moment of our love making is precious. I want his love making and those moments for me; for always; just for me.

"I'm in love with Josh. I mean it's love beyond film performance love. It's real love. It's more than a physical thing with us. He feels it too. I know he does. I just love everything about him, and I totally love making love with him. We always have such beautiful sex together. He plunges his huge thirsty organ deep down into my

nectar well; and he stays inside my flower, locked deeply inside me, feeling my heat, immersed in my nectar. You know, in girl-talk ways, what I mean, don't you, Bertie?"

"Sure, I do, sweet baby. Bertie knows. Bertie will get him back. And I know how to do it. I just had an idea. We're going to perform that scene where you are making love with one of your partners. You know, the scene where you are moving like a wild, craven, sex-addicted wildcat, twerking and gyrating like crazy on your partner's penis; and his penis is stroking inside you, and you take charge?"

"Yes. You mean where I place my fingers on his penis and start rapidly stroking it while it's still thrusting into my vagina; and when the penis starts shooting, I pull it out of me and it shoots over my mons; but then I reinsert it into my vagina. I continue fucking like I'm a wild mink in heat; and his penis continues shooting inside me; and then, when it's spent, I pull his penis out of me and I suck it while I smile to the cameras? You mean that scene?"

"Yes Marty, that's the scene. We're going to do that again; only this time you will have two partners, initially. While you are, again, boinking, twerking, and grating on the penis like you're a wild mink, and while one partner's penis is stroking you vagina, you will also be licking and sucking your second partner's penis. Do you believe you can do that without losing concentration on twerking and gyrating your vagina?"

"Yes, Bertie. I'm positive I can do that. I've done it before. The only thing that's new is the part where my fingers accelerate the ejaculation of the penis inside my vagina, and the pulling out and reinserting movements. But I'm sure I can hold my concentration on both penises."

"Good, Marty. Well, we'll do different takes and use different partners if we need to. I want you to practice until you get it right. And I don't care what it costs. We don't care what it cost, do we George?"

George shook his head. *"No, we don't care what it costs."*

"Marty, after your first partner has finished ejaculating inside your vagina, we're going to have you pivot your pelvis and your vagina towards your second partner. And with your second partner, you're going to perform an identical fornication scene, Maiden position. You're going to, again, twerk and gyrate upon your second partner's penis like you are a sex crazed nympho wildcat. You're going to smile a starry-eyed smile the whole time, showing the cameras that you love making love so much that you can never get enough of it. Are you following me? Can you do that?"

"Yes, Bertie. I'm following. And yes, I can do that. And with my second partner, I only need to concentrate on pleasuring my vagina. I will not be simultaneously performing fellatio with another penis, is that right?"

"Yes, you've got it. Now, after your second partner has ejaculated that first spurt onto your mons; and after you have reinserted his penis in your vagina and he has finished coming; and you've taken his penis out of your vagina, you are going to stand up. At that point, your two partners will stand with you. You will take turns with them; kissing them; pressing your body close to theirs, while they place their hands on your ass and squeeze it; and while you hold their penises in your hands and gently stroke them. Can you do that?"

"Sure, Bertie. That's easy."

"Good Marty. Well, I think you'll love this next part. At this point, a third partner will walk into the bedroom. He will have a very huge penis, about three inches longer and half again as fat in circumference as the penises of your first two partners. When your first two partners see him, they will automatically stand aside and apart from you. Your third partner will then take you into his arms and hold you close to him and begin kissing your mouth; and you will grasp his penis and begin slowly stroking it. You will be all smiles

and giggles because you will recognize this third partner. You will kiss him wildly because you truly do love this man."

"And who will he be, Bertie?"

"Josh. And he will love you for being the sex obsessed nymph that you are!"

"You've got him, already? You've got Josh for me?"

"Yes. I told you: we're going to do whatever it takes, whatever it costs, to make you the world's most adored, most notorious, most desired goddess of intimate artistry."

"I don't know how to thank you, Bertie." Tears flowed from Marty's eyes; happy, joyous, grateful tears.

"I'm not finished. There's more. After you and Josh have hugged and kissed and fondled each other, you will return to the bed and assume the Maiden position. Josh will kneel beside you. You will lick his penis in your most loving, lavish manner; showing the cameras that you are in awe of his enormous penis. You will then spend considerable time kissing and licking the head of his penis. The, Josh will perform some cunnilingus with you, to get you prepared for intercourse. Finally, Josh will hold his penis head against your outer vaginal lips and begin to penetrate you. And then we will cut the film scene and stop filming."

"You mean I don't get to make love with Josh? I don't get to make love with the love of my life?"

"Not in that film; not at this time. The cameras will do a fade away from your vagina as you are just about to make love with Josh. Lettering will appear which says:

'MORE TO COME'

"Then what?" asked Marty.

"Then we will take some time to relax and prepare you and Josh for your second film in that two-film sequence."

"Where will we go? Where will Josh go?"

"Marty, sweetheart, this is going to be a Bertie production. We'll do all the filming right here in our mansion. You and Josh will retire to the West wing. You'll have the master bedroom suite in the West wing, with its California King bed and its full bath with its oversized tub and shower and outdoor jacuzzi. Its French doors open to the deck of our heated swimming pool. You should be comfortable there. I want you and Josh to be completely relaxed before we shoot the second film of the series."

"But Bertie, don't misunderstand me. I'm very grateful that you're going to set me up for a night with Josh. I'm sure we'll make sweet love. I'm very grateful; but you'll be paying Josh's agency rates. My twenty-four hours with Josh will cost you ten thousand dollars, easily."

"Don't worry about how we spend our money, sweetheart. You are like a daughter to us, and we don't care what it costs, do we George?" Bertie hugged Marty and smiled into her eyes.

"We don't care what it costs," said George.

"I want to create in Josh's mind that he is very fortunate to have the love interest of such a wonderful woman as you, Marty. I'm thinking he should spend some time with you; really get to know you. I think the two of you should have time together and do some things together; kind of like having a honeymoon together. That way, when Josh performs with you in that third film, I think he'll make love with you like he knows and appreciates that you truly are a goddess; and that he is truly blessed to be your lover.

"And I think you should become better acquainted with the mansion house. George and I have the East wing. There's a North wing, where our helpers stay. There's Smith, Gracey, and Emmy. When you need something, push button three on your bedroom phone. That gets you Smith. When you want something from the kitchen, press button four. Tell Gracey what you want and she'll make it for you.

She has a fully stocked freezer, fridge, and pantry. And when you want to be massaged or have your hair coiffed, or your makeup put on by a real pro, press button five. Emmy will take care of everything.

"I think you and Josh should tell Smith that you want to go horse-back riding. He'll press some buttons that move the wind shields and nets on our tennis courts underground and convert the courts into a helicopter pad. A chopper will come and take you and George to our Front Range Ranch, where Birch, our ranch foreman, will have your horses saddled and waiting for you. I think you and Josh should let Birch guide you into the low mountains on horse to a beautiful waterfall on the creek that runs though our property. I hope you and Josh will make love there. It's a beautiful, memorable spot. Isn't it, George?"

"It is," said George.

"But Bertie, a whole week with Josh will easily cost you seventy thousand dollars!"

"We want you to be happy, Baby. We want you to think of yourself as our own daughter, okay, Baby? And we don't care what it costs, do we George?" Bertie hugged Marty and kissed her cheek.

"We don't care what it costs," said George, shrugging his shoulders.

"I don't know what to say."

"Oh, I almost forgot! On your pillow, Marty, you will find an envelope that says 'Marty.' In the envelope you will find a platinum-colored credit card with your name on it. It has a credit limit of five hundred thousand dollars. I suggest that you and Josh go shopping at some of the Chi-Chi boutiques in Boulder and Cherry Creek North. What I'd like you to purchase are items that show off your spectacular breasts and your spectacular derriere. We're going to outfit you in reveal wear. I'm thinking tops that allow your breasts to spill out when you twist your body or lean forward; and I'm thinking mini skirts that reveal your vagina and derriere when

you stretch, bend over, or lift a leg to ascend a staircase. Are you following me?"

"I don't know how I'll ever be able to thank the two of you. You are so wonderful to me. I love you both."

"You don't have to thank us, Marty. We love you. That's all. We just love you. Now, I want to let the paparazzi know where you will be so they can capture photos of you and your love interest, Josh while you are shopping. I want you to frequently kiss him and place your hand over his penis. And I want him to frequently grope you and squeeze your bare ass with his hands. If you two will remember to be touchy, feely, that will help promote your second film of that two-part series. I'm thinking I'll call it: 'THIRD TIME'S A CHARM,' because Josh will be your third and last partner for the two films.

"And in the third film, I want you to do the same wildcat twerks and gyrations with Josh inside you as with the other two partners. But after you have pulled out his penis and reinserted it, I want you to have extended lovemaking with him. I want the two of you kissing and hugging; and him getting hard all over again; and a seemingly endless scene of the two of you touching and hugging and kissing. Are you okay with that? Are you okay with me using Josh for your third partner; or would you rather I get someone else?"

"No one else, Bertie. Josh. It has to be Josh. I want him. He's so special and so wonderful with me. Thank you, Bertie. I need him. I love him. I know he loves me. He never wants to pull out of me. He loves staying inside me. I know he loves being close to me. I think he'd stay in me forever if he could hold back his ejaculations. He has such an amazing, loving penis. It always feels so good and natural inside me. When it's inside me, I feel like I'm finally home where I belong. He makes me feel so peaceful and safe and appreciated. It's a happiness I can't describe. It's hard to imagine how sex could get any better than having the one penis inside me that totally under-stands my body. And I love sucking him; running my teeth over the

top of his penis, thrilling him like that; and closing my lips over his shaft while I'm pulling up on his shaft, like letting him know that my mouth is givning him the most wonderful fellatio, ever. Our sex so incredibly beautiful. I want it to go on forever. I can never get enough of Josh."

"Have you ever felt like that about your other lovers?"

"Which ones do you mean?"

"Oh, your past seductions; the twins, Darren, the four J's, your geometry teacher. I'm just trying to understand your nymphomania so I know the best way to brand you. Do you ever call those men to see how they are doing? Do you ever get back together with any of them? I mean, while you were romantically entwined with them, while you were making love with them, didn't you feel the same ways with them as you now feel about Josh? You basically left all those men. I'm just trying to know how your mind works, Marty."

"Well, I suppose I did. It's kind of like meeting someone on a trip. You play a while, have fun; then move on. I guess I wasn't looking for permanence and neither were they."

"They weren't?"

"No, I don't think so. Not really. The twins were looking to hustle me and Maria for a good time; take the boredom out of their senior high school year. My teacher had issues with his wife. He had a lack of sex and anger thing. He used me to get back at her, that's all. Darren definitely used me to punish Carol. And we did. We drove her insane. The four J's were into their macho cult thinking. Having me around for ready sex boosted their bravado. But Vietnam took all that out of them when it took their lives. Carl used me. He still does. But we use each other. We both know we do, and we don't care. It's an understanding sort of thing. It's a physical attraction, physical addiction thing. That's complicated; but that's all it is. Part of it was

to punish his wife for being such a control freak. Then, she died, so that stopped.

"But the other part of Carl is his sex obsession over me. That seems to be ongoing with Carl and me. It's a mutual thing. We both have the obsession. We respect that about each other. When Carl needs to have me, or when I need to have him, we find ways to get together. My Premium Service members are mostly about escapism from other relationships. And that would include you and George trying to cope with the loss of your daughter. I'm very sorry about that. I truly am."

"Thank you, Marty. But what about you?"

"What about me?"

"You. I need to unwrap you. I need to understand your nympho component. If it's sex, per se, then why don't you go back to the men you've had great sex with before? Why don't you see your former teacher? Why don't you see the twins or Darren?"

"You could ask that about a lot of my porn partners, too. It's what drives me. It's not just the sex. It's more about that I have to make a new seduction. I need that next conquest. I need to continually prove to myself that I can capture that next man. By that, I mean bed him; come between him and his significant other; displace the other woman; wreck his marriage, if I can. I guess the best way I can describe it is my elevator dream. I live that dream. I can't get off and leave my dark room and go with the normal people. I need to stay on the elevator and ride it to the next room where the new penises are. I can't go back to the room I was just in."

"Is that your driver, then? Does it have an anger component? I mean, are you trying to lash out; retaliate against your abandonment and the way those WEX girls and their mothers shunned you?"

"Yeah, maybe. But I think it's more like picking up new stones and dropping old ones, like I did when I walked the WEX driveway by myself, picking up pebbles and dropping them. Once I drop an old pebble, I don't go back to it because there are so many new ones. And I need to tell myself that a new one loves me. Once I take all the love I can get from a pebble, I drop it."

"Why must you drop it?"

"Because I need much more love than one pebble can give me. I can't carry all the pebbles around with me, so I just drop old ones and pick up new ones. The driveway is full of pebbles. The world is full of men. I can't stop getting new ones. And I don't want to stop. Getting new ones eases the pain of what Mother did to me."

"Thank you, Marty. That helps me a lot. But, Marty," conjectured Bertie, "you seem to feel the same way about Marshawn as you do about Josh. And then there's your attractions to Bob and Carl. Are you starting to come out of your addiction? I mean are you thinking you'll settle down with one of them?"

"I don't know. If I did, it would have to be Bob, or possibly David."

"David? The man who runs the firm you work at?"

"Yes, possibly. We're close friends, but we've never had sex. It's complicated. He's complicated. Our relationship is complicated. I really don't want to talk about him."

"Then we won't. But I thought I was seeing something incredibly special when you were on set with Marshawn. I kept thinking to myself that the two of you had discovered your true loves. I even envisioned the two of you getting married."

"No Bertie. That's not going to happen. That would ruin everything; take all the excitement out of it."

"But I thought when you were on set with Marshawn, you acted even more like a vixen than you did with Josh. There was so much energy going on between you two. It was the most uninhibited, salacious foreplay sequence I've ever witnessed."

"That's because I was in my seduction mindset, Bertie. I was picking up a stone. I go all out to get the stone I want. You really thought that foreplay segment was that good?"

"Oh, Marty, yes, I surely did. There you were, naked with your arms around Marshawn's neck, stroking his neck and the back of his head while you were French kissing him. You pressed your body against his. The camera shoots to his wide wedding band. Clearly, you were being a shameless coveter. You were consciously stealing Marshawn from his wife. If you knew the hurts you caused her, you certainly didn't let her feelings stop you. You had no misgivings about your lust. You unleashed your uninhibited promiscuity. You took the hand that held his wedding ring and moved it right to your vagina, while you continued French kissing him and stroking his head. You pushed your yearning breasts firmly against his chest, while you guided his first three fingers, including his wedding ring finger, into your vagina. You wanted to take his wedding ring into your vagina to symbolize that you intended to destroy his marriage with your vagina, didn't you?"

"Yes, honestly, yes. That's exactly what I was doing. I love doing that. It's my mental way of having him accept my lust; having him accept the fact that my intent is for my vagina to devour his marriage; having him honor my intent. By letting me help him pleasure me with his ring finger, he was signaling me that he was willing to facilitate my intent; letting me know that he was willing to help me destroy his marriage. He symbolically joined me. We were being wicked, together. The two of us were metaphorically fucking his marriage."

"I knew it. My erotic, naughty girl meter went crazy. I felt you were signaling to your viewers that you were ravaging his soul with your kisses, while absorbing his marriage within your vagina. It was the most magnificently done, passionate seduction scene I've ever

seen you perform. No other porn star has ever heated up the screen the way you did that day."

"Do you really think so? You're not just saying that?"

"Yes, I believe what I'm saying. I could feel the heat coming off the screen. What were you feeling?"

"Oh, that I loved him, and I wanted him. That I felt for his situation; that I wanted to take him from his wife; that I didn't care about destroying his family; that satisfying my passion was more important than any moral considerations. I was trying to communicate through my kisses to him that our love was much more important than any ridiculous concept of morality."

"Well, whatever was happening, it was breathtaking and beautiful. You had this intensity about making love with Marshawn. You were throwing off a feverish heat. I could feel how much you craved making love with him. What was happening in your off-screen lives when you made that film?"

"Oh, that gets into some deep psychological stuff, Bertie. It gets all blended together with my nymphomania. Sometimes it swirls around inside me. It starts with me realizing how our time together in this life is precious; and then it intensifies. I start feeling like I need to love Marshawn like he's the only man left on planet earth; like civilization will end if I stop making love with him.

"When we're together we fall into this other world. Then I just go insanely head over heels into love with Marshawn. I feel like humanity will end if my passions ever ease up; but then the pure erotic joys of having sexual intercourse with him take over my entire mind and body. It's those raw sexual thrills of having his phenomenal, gorgeous penis and his tongue inside me. He sends me into ecstasy; then I can't stop our lovemaking until I collapse from exhaustion. I love resting my head on his chest afterwards, while I continue stroking his penis. It never ceases to amaze me. It's so huge! I can't get enough

of him, Bertie. I love him." Marty shrugged her shoulders, hoping to cut off Bertie's probe.

"Marty, do those feelings have something to do with Marshawn being a black man?" Bertie wasn't about to withdraw her inquiry. She was a good coach. She needed to understand what helped her performer attain her optimum. Marty understood Bertie well enough by now to know that a fluffy softball answer would only lead to more questions. Only a full explanation would satisfy Bertie:

"Yes, Bertie, black has everything to do with those feelings. It makes it that much more special, knowing that I, a beautiful white woman, am stealing an exceptionally handsome black man away from his black wife. It's complicated. It started a few years ago when my Hispanic friend, Rita, convinced me I should join her in an orgy with seven black basketball players. I had already started doing some prostitution; but I was only doing white college boys and a few white salesmen. It had never occurred to me to cross the racial boundary. The thought had never even come up. I had reservations when Rita approached me with her offer. I had fears that black men would get rough with me, or that their penises would stretch me, or tear me and hurt me. I feared getting abused, too. I honestly believed that blacks had hostility towards whites; and I was afraid they'd take that out on me.

"Rita insisted I was totally wrong. She convinced me to go with her to an orgy and to try having sex with blacks, at least one time. Also, Rita opined, that as a white girl, I needed to atone for the atrocity of slavery. She laid this guilt trip on me, like I owned a plantation or something. She convinced me I had some kind of unspoken civic duty to end racial division by having sex with black men. She told me that every time we white women make love with black men, we help them erase their inherited emotional scars. She convinced me that having sex with black men was the morally correct and patriotic thing for patriotic white American girls to do.

"Well, was I pleasantly surprised? You bet I was! After my first orgy experience with black men, I became a woman on a mission. I came to believe that interracial sex with black men was my civic duty. My orgy with those black men opened a whole new perspective. I took immense pride in what I was doing. I, sweet innocent Marty Mallory, was healing America's racial divide. That night I gave those basketball players the most enthusiastic fucking and sucking I had ever performed in my career up to that point. And, I learned a valuable lesson about love making that night. I learned that black men are sensational sex partners. Most of my black partners are more loving than most of my white partners.

"After Marshawn and I became lovers, I asked him straight out why black men were better lovers than white men. I expected a flip answer. But instead, I got an education on black history. Marshawn told me I have slavery to thank. He said from 1619 until 1863, two hundred forty-four years, American blacks were slaves to American whites. During that twelve-generation span of time, entire African villages were captured for shipment as slaves to the Americas. Often, the slave traders offered the slaves in entire village lots. The slave shippers would essentially buy a group lot, which included the weaker and more unattractive blacks. That was problematic for the slave shippers.

"Only the strongest blacks were desired to work the fields on Caribbean and American plantations. Only the strongest and most beautiful of the captured African women were desired for breeding additional slaves and for the sexual pleasures of white plantation owners. The slave shippers couldn't make money on weak men or undesirable women. Marshawn reminded me that these captured blacks were considered property; not people. They were no more valuable than the grains or hogs that were also carried on the slave ships. The weak and unattractive blacks were considered inferior goods, much like spoiled grain or diseased animals. This

situation provided the backdrop for a process that accelerated nat-
ural selection.

"Marshawn explained that the slave ships only carried enough
rations for two out of every three slave captives that they took on
board in Africa. Shippers sought to maximize their profits by deliv-
ering as many strong men and beautiful black women as possible.
During the first week of oceanic transit, the shippers quickly discov-
ered which blacks had the greatest stamina for the long voyage. The
sick, the weak, and the unattractive blacks were singled out. The
slave traders were not about to waste their meat and grain feeding
these undesirables. They were not going to get money for them in
the American slave markets. So, the inferior slaves' hands were tied;
their feet were roped onto a line of rope, as many as fifty people
tied to one line of rope; and the rope line was secured to bag of lead
cannon balls. The cannon balls and the inferior goods blacks were
tossed overboard. These inferior people became drowning victims.
Shark food. This cost cutting process accelerated natural selection.
Only the strongest, most beautiful blacks with the greatest stamina
reached the western hemisphere.

"When Marshawn first explained this practice of the slave ship-
pers, I was horrified. I thought the Spanish, English and Portuguese
monarchies that encouraged the slave trade were hideous rulers.
What they encouraged and condoned was a repulsive, criminal
genocide by today's standards. I felt sorry for those who lost their
lives, dragged to the ocean's bottom, in such a horrible way. I still feel
sorry for them, hundreds of years later.

"But I have refined my thoughts about it. It was normal human
inhuman behavior by shippers whose minds believed that the blacks
were property; not real people. Their inhumane belief system accel-
erated natural selection. I see that history's sordid chapter of black
slavery has ultimately inured to the benefit of my libido. Through
those culling's at sea and many subsequent generations of selective

breeding on the plantations, this accelerated selection has brought me the most fabulous porn partners, with the most magnificent penises in the entire world! I'm terribly selfish and hopelessly self-centered to think this way, I know; but it's the truth! Because of slavery, I now get to make love with the strongest, handsomest porn partners, who all have fabulous penises!

"So, you see, Bertie, I consider myself fantastically blessed and grateful for those centuries of slave trade. My black porn partners are beautiful, strong men with fantastic stamina. They have spectacular, splendid penises. They are descendants of extremely sensitive and nuanced forebearers, who had to adapt and be intelligent and compliant to survive. Thanks to slavery, I have the benefit of love making with my wonderful black male porn partners. They are sensitive, loving, imminently pliable, nuanced, and accommodating. They are, heart and soul, dedicated to pleasing me. Bertie. They are fabulous lovers. They stretch me; they pleasure my entire vagina; reach everywhere inside me; and please me, endlessly, with beautiful orgasms. They impart their passions for love making to me, and gratefully receive my passions in return. In short, Bertie, I love making love with my well-hung black partners. I feel deliriously happy and joyful while I'm making love with them; and I always feel blessed to be having sex with them. I can never get enough black dicks. I will never tire of making porn films with black partners. I love them and I appreciate why they are such wonderful lovers.

"Did you know, Bertie, that, after Lincoln's 1863 emancipation proclamation, blacks were still pseudo-slaves to whites until the Civil Rights Act of 1964 and the end of the South's Jim Crow laws? They endured another ninety-nine years of being considered an underclass people. In America they suffered three hundred forty-three years as underclass people; and now, since 1964's civil rights act, they have also endured discriminatory red lining lending and zoning practices; and determined efforts to suppress their votes.

They've endured misguided zealots' efforts, like the Planned Parenthood wackos, to abort their beautiful babies; criminal gangs' efforts to addict their children with drugs; and their children made to suffer inferior educations because they've been denied school choice for their kids. They often get lower wages for the same jobs, and less advancement opportunities. The ways they have suffered and the ways they still suffer are endless. We owe them a collective apology and an atonement, Bertie. We must feel the shames of our ancestors. They've been wronged.

"Bertie, here's the other reason why blacks are the best lovers. It's more than their physical attributes. Many blacks have become accustomed to trying harder than white people. Among them are many who are so accustomed to serving white people that many of them have developed the attitude that they must do better than a white to even become noticed or appreciated. That attitude carries over to their love making. They're consistently the best lovers that they can possibly be. Discrimination has brought out the best of them, Bertie. I feel it while I make love with them on my sets. They earnestly want to please me. They are tireless, patient, caring lovers. I totally love making love with them. As a white woman, I feel it's upon me to make the very best porn with them that I possibly can; to totally love them; to help make up for all the slights they've had throughout history. Our attitudes complement. We experience freedom of attitudes while we copulate. I feel a sense of rapture while I'm doing a black partner. It's beautiful.

"They've mastered the artistic nuances of erotic love making, Bertie. Partly due to their accelerated natural selection and partly due to our complementary attitudes, they are my best porn partners. Black men make me feel loved with an intensity that reaches into my primal roots. When I make love with them, I feel their love deeply within me. They have this crying need to give exceptional love making to a woman. It's so much more than sex. I definitely notice

it. They crave intimacy. They need to give and receive that erotic, romantic closeness. I notice it. That makes me want to reciprocate it.

"I become so intensely intimate with my black partners that I gush inside. I have more than my normal orgasm flows. I have volcanic explosions. They're gush rushes; internal damn breaks. It's the most beautiful sex. I become emotively obsessed when I'm having sex with a black man. I'm touched so deeply while making love with black men that I lose all thoughts; other than that, I feel I must love my black partner like he and I are the only two humans in the universe; like the future of humanity depends upon the intensity and sincerity of our performance.

"My black lover partner becomes my link to humanity; and I need that link to feel like I'm a complete human. I feel I must give him every measure of all the love I have within me. Our ancestors needed to discover that feeling to procreate, to get civilization started. Blacks call it soul. My black lovers have soul, Bertie. Their soul reaches out to my soul; theirs lifts my soul right out of my conscious mind and places it inside my blood. My vagina feels a beautiful blood surge from making love with a black soul. That surge fires everything inside me.

"And, blacks have got size, Bertie!" Marty's eyes were expressively wide as saucers. Her enthusiasm bubbled: *"Oh, Bertie, I do so much love their size. I truly do! I shamelessly admit it. I love their magnificent, huge, beautiful penises. I can never get enough of them, Bertie. They have the most fabulous penises. It's breathtaking to have them inside me. I just love it; I mean, I totally love all of it. When I have a huge black penis inside me, I find myself praising God that I chose to become an adult film actress. Having that huge penis working its magical thrusts inside me makes me realize that being an erotic film star is the greatest, most wonderful, most emotionally satisfying career path in the world. I can't imagine not having black penises available to satisfy my sexual cravings, whenever I want*

them. I don't know how any woman can live without having access to a black penis. It's the ultimate pacifier; better than any drug; and so addictive! I feel sorry for women who have never experienced the wonder of it. Knowing what I know now, being denied access to black penises would drive me insane.

"Honestly, Bertie, speaking as a woman who's performed hundreds of adult film scenes, there's simply no comparison between a white, seven-inch-long, one-inch diameter penis; and a black, ten inch or twelve inch long, hard, anxious, and loving to please, three-inch diameter penis. I understand how my vagina adapts to the penis that's inside it and the anatomical explanation for it and all that; but trust me on this, Bertie:

"A black penis knows how to play inside baseball. I mean, inside a woman baseball. They touch every one of the bases, all the time; and they stay on base for the longest time. They rub along my clit, constantly stimulating me, all the time. They stroke my walls, sending hot sensory flashes through my entire network of clitoral tentacles; and all the way down into my loins, all the time. They stay firm for me, all the time. When I have a black penis inside me, I feel dominated and controlled and transformed into a man's woman; like a woman wants to feel dominated while she's loved by a real man, Bertie.

"Yeah, I went black during Rita's orgy night, Bertie. I fell into the sexual wonderland of black penises, and I've been falling further and deeper into that wonderful place, ever since. Those basketball players opened my eyes to what sensational erotic feelings are attainable during sex. Those men stretched my limbic mind. They took me to places beyond any place my sensuality had ever gone before. And they lit a fire to my innermost cravings and feelings. I never appreciated how wonderful making love could be; or how much I loved sex, until that night. I am so thankful to Rita for opening me up to that wonderful world. That was my first time

to experience having all of everything wonderful. I had penises in both my hands; and penises inside me; penises everywhere. I loved my erotic surges so much that I begged those men to book me again. I begged Rita to book me for more orgy events with visiting players; and now I feel so blessed to be one of Rita's regulars.

"I think that was the night that tripped me into the world I know now, where love making has become my obsession. It was a magical night for me. Yes, Bertie, I'm proud to tell the whole world that I've gone black, and I've never gone back. I often fall asleep dreaming that I have my arms wrapped around a huge black penis and I'm kissing its head. Black penises are like that for me. They stay alive, hard, and firm, inside my head. I'm always receptive to making porn with black lovers.

"Oh, don't misunderstand me, Bertie. I have many white lovers and our love making is fantastic; and the love of my life and the one I want to share my life with is Bob; and Carl is my go-to man for fabulous sex, because of the ways his mind and penis know how to live inside my body. But, if given the choice between a black partner and a white partner; and both were unknown to me from performing previously with me, I'll choose the black partner, every time.

"Most of all, I love holding a black penis in my hands, putting my lips on it, and kissing it. Just touching that huge penis and thinking about the fun I'll have with it and how it's going to love filling up the inside of me and pleasuring me is an immense source of joy for me, Bertie. It validates my life as a whole woman. It confirms that my choices to become a prostitute, make films and perform in orgies, were all good choices. I feel like that at the very beginning of every foreplay with a black performer, because I am certain that sex with him will be fabulous. I get excited and hot and wet inside, just holding his penis; before I even start kissing and sucking it. I love stroking it and imagining how wonderful it's going to feel when it first penetrates my vagina's inner lips.

"I'm now addicted to interracial sex, Bertie. I love when I'm placed in a scene where my director wants me to suck and fuck black cocks for an entire hour, or longer. If I had to write down my career goals on a job application, I would have to write sucking and fucking black penises, twenty-four hours a day, seven days a week, for the rest of my life. I love making love with black men. I love kissing them and rubbing my hands on their chests.

"But there's a troublesome, adverse aspect to my cravings for black lovers, Bertie. Some black men prefer a white woman to a black woman. They see a white woman as a status symbol. As a highly ranked porn actress who does interracial porn, I am especially prized by many blacks as a status symbol. I've become an attraction magnet for some of them. I naturally love making love with them. And it thrills me to convert them into my steady lovers.

"But here's what gets me into trouble. I feel deliciously wicked about unsettling their families. That especially satisfies me, because I reassure myself that my immorality has a stronger hold on those men's' feelings than the religious messaging they hear at home and in church. The black churches have a powerful hold on many black men. They preach regular reminders not to sin and to be good husbands and fathers. That presents a bit of a challenge for me. I must work extra hard to convert those men to my immoral ways. But I keep trying. I never give up on a seduction, once I've started one. I feel I must set them free, for real.

"Several black women have sent me hate mail for causing them to lose their husbands' love. I understand how they feel; but I don't care. I don't obey religious commandments or morality codes. When people tell me what I am doing is terribly, morally wrong, I simply ignore them. I know what I'm doing is right for me. When I date a black man, I'm know I could be causing a black woman considerable agony. She intuits that I'll almost certainly make love with 'her man.' And she's right about that. Also, she fears she may lose him to

me. She knows she can't do anything to prevent that. And she's right about that, too.

"Aaliyah, Marshawn's wife, knows I often earn twice the money in one day that she earns in an entire year. Ironically, Marshawn now spends his income on me; so, she's forced to work two extra jobs to make ends meet. While she's waiting tables and scrubbing floors, I'm making love with her husband. I love the arrangement. She curses me and my wantonness; calls me a sinful, immoral whore; but she's unable to stop me. She knows I'll use Marshawn for my sexual gratification, until I've had my fill of him; and that, eventually, I'll likely move on to another man when Marshawn's films with me stop selling well. Porn is like professional sports that way. Players get traded and cut from teams. It's business. But Aaliyah also understands that Marshawn may never feel the same love for her afterwards. That's likely gone forever. He may seek to spend his life as one of my loves; or possibly with some other promiscuous white women. He may possibly pursue whiteness to distance himself from his race. That possibility horrifies her. She knows I've turned her life upside down. She also knows I don't care.

"What she doesn't know is how much I love to psychologically torture her. When Marshawn makes love with me, have you noticed how I put my hands on his face while I kiss him? Have you noticed how I hold his muscular back and shoulders while he thrusts into me and while I lift my hips and gyrate my vagina to meet his thrusts and give his penis more stimulation? Have you paid attention to how I throw my head back and giggle and laugh, open mouthed; and how I say things? Like:

'I love the way you're doing to me; Oh, Marshawn, that feels so wonderful. Don't stop, baby. Keep going baby. Yes baby. I'm coming now. Oh, yes. That's so beautiful. Won't you please come inside me and tell me you love me? You do love me, don't you baby? Say

you love me. I need to hear it. Yes! I love hearing you say that. Tell me you'll always love me. Yes! I love you when you say that. Come inside me baby. Yes. I want you to. That's it. I feel you. Kiss me. Yes. Kiss me. Tell me you love that I'm an immoral whore. Tell me that I'm the only woman you've always wanted. Yes. I love hearing you saying those things to me. I love you, too, Marshawn.'

"I'm especially tender and loving with Marshawn because I know Aaliyah watches our films. She must like to torture herself. I do my part by making films that haunt her and drive her out of her mind. That makes her bitchy and intolerable. Marshawn can't stand Aaliyah when she gets like that. He leaves her and comes to me. I'd like him to get divorced from her.

"Aaliyah's trapped on her personal rat wheel. She can't change the way her mind works. She can't stop obsessing over her religion and her bibles. She can't pry her mind away from her fears of going to hell if she does the things with Marshawn that he and I so freely do. She can no longer make Marshawn go to her church and bible studies with her. Since he's been seeing me privately, he refuses to attend church. Poor, poor Aaliyah! She cannot change her skin color. I know she hates hates her situation. Marshawn has told me everything. She blames everything on me. She says it's my fault for making her life a living hell.

"But it's not my fault. It's her own culture's fault. I just love making love with Marshawn, that's all. Aaliyah can't imagine or rationalize why Marshawn would want to leave her and their children to spend every moment he possibly can with an incorrigibly bad woman, like me. She can't comprehend the allure of freedom.

"Poor Marshawn. He gets confused about his situation sometimes. He told me he was visited by two women from his wife's church. They told him he should feel ashamed about being with me. I was amused to hear about that confrontation.

"Does this make you feel ashamed to be with me, I asked him, as I French kissed him."

"No," he replied.

"Well, does this make you feel ashamed to be with me," I asked him as I rubbed my nipple over his lips. Again, he assured me that that did not make him ashamed to be with me.

"How about this? Does this make you ashamed to be with me?' I asked him while I kissed his penis and ran my tongue over its head. Again, he assured me that my doing a sinful, adulterous thing like that did not make him ashamed of me.

"As I rubbed his penis against my inner vaginal lips and inserted it into me, I again questioned him whether he felt any shame; any shame at all, about being with me. He again assured me that he felt no shame when he was with me, no matter how immoral I was. Then we made beautiful love.

"Marshawn,' I explained, 'when women notice a man is wearing a wedding ring, they assume he belongs to the woman who gave him that ring. Those church women who called on you thought you were being unfaithful to your ring partner. And they believed they were entitled to shame you."

"But, Marty, I love you. I don't love my wife. I've never loved her. We were married because our families knew each other; that's all." Marshawn was sheepish and embarrassed.

"Sweetheart, when you make love with a woman, it's very unusual to wear another woman's wedding ring. It makes your lover feel unimportant. Have you ever thought about how my feelings while we make love; knowing you are wearing your wife's ring?"

"My eyes searched his. I wondered if they held a hidden truth, or if my feelings were something he simply hadn't thought about. He didn't answer me.

"But the following day he called me. He was in his car outside my house. He asked me to get in his car. He wanted to take me

someplace. We went to his bank, where he withdrew every penny that he had from his bank accounts. Then we went to a jeweler. He plunked down his $72,000 savings, his $6,000 cash value from his life insurance policy, and his wedding ring.

"I want you to create a butterfly out of gold," he told the jeweler. "I want you to melt the gold in this wedding ring to help supply the gold for her butterfly. Put tiny rubies on the butterfly's wingtips and put three larger rubies, the largest my money will buy, for the body of the butterfly. I want you to use 24 caret gold, too, the best you have for jewelry. Take a good look at this lady, mister. This butterfly will land on a neckless right above her beautiful breasts; so, make a butterfly that looks special on her because she is special."

"I was taken aback. I have received far more expensive gifts, but this was all the money Marshawn had in the entire world. He and Aaliyah had been scrimping and saving to make a down payment on a larger house for their family. He was giving me all the wealth they had; surrendering the insurance security for his family; and leaving Aaliyah and his children with nothing. He was declaring his love for me in the most honest, straightforward way any man ever had. Whenever we're out together, I wear a gold chain. His butterfly pendant rests right above my cleavage. It's elegant beyond words. Knowing it includes the gold from his wedding ring makes it the most priceless gift any man has ever given me. I wear it whenever we make love. I also wear it while I'm creating my porn films because it perfectly furthers my image.

"Marshawn, sweetheart," I asked, "How will you feel, seeing me wear your butterfly while I perform with other partners, and during my orgy films? I will have other men's penises in my mouth and vagina. You need to understand that I'm going to continue being a ravenous whore and porn star. I love your gift; but that does not entitle you to believe you own me. I expect to create hundreds more erotic films and have sex with possibly hundreds more Premium

Members. I'll be seen in public places with many of them. You cannot be jealous when you see me on a magazine cover wearing your neckless, while I'm kissing another man with my hand on his penis. You'll have to accept me for who I am, Marshawn. I'm an incorrigible, immoral whore. You need to know that."

"Marty, I gave it to you," he said. "It's my gift of love; from me, for you. You wear it whenever you wish to wear it. Why are you saying these things? I love seeing you making love. I understand how much you need to do that. I really do."

"Well, would it make you angry to see me making love with other men and sucking them while wearing your gift of love? I'm asking because it's so beautiful and it perfectly complements my butterfly tattoo. I think it will enhance my film image; make my performances that much more memorable and erotic, don't you?"

"Oh, yes, definitely. It will enhance your image. You'll be the ultimate erotic butterfly. Your butterfly will be recognizable as the brand of the world's ultimate erotic actress. The whole world will adore you. They'll salivate over your insatiable vagina. And I'll feel highly honored, seeing you wearing my butterfly while you perform."

"You really do love me that much, don't you Marshawn? I mean you really won't feel any jealousy, will you?"

"No, I don't think so. I know what you do. I know you love creating intimate film. I know you love having new lovers. I know you immerse yourself in immoral sex. I know sex is your life. That's you, Marty. I knew that about you before I performed with you our first time. Knowing all that about you, I can only feel love for you. I know every woman needs honest love; and you're no different. Will you still love me while you're performing? That's all I want to know."

"Of course, I will, Marshawn. I promise I'll always kiss your gold butterfly as my good luck omen before I put another man's penis inside my mouth or my vagina. That will remind me how special

you are, okay? When you see a film of me performing intimately with other partners, you'll know I'm thinking of you. Okay, baby?"

"Okay, thanks Marty, that's really sweet of you. I'll be very happy knowing my gift will help your brand image. I love you, Marty. You've taught me so much about life and love. I will love you forever."

"Marshawn, you're much too sweet. You know I'm completely immoral. You know I have other lovers and that I'll have others in the future, don't you?"

"I know all that. You've told me before. I truly do understand. Honest I do. I just want you to know I love you deeply and totally. Understand that I'll always have feel-good love for you. Know my love is with you while you perform. I'll feel happiness for you. Honest I will." Marshawn's eyes were honest. I knew he meant what he said."

"We made sweet love that afternoon. Marshawn feels no shame about loving me. The world is full of people who believe they know what's best for others. But Marshawn has broken free of them. I'm proud of him. He wants only the best for me, even though I'm obsessed with my sex work. That's true love. Unfortunately, our love has created a terrible dilemma for Aaliyah, Bertie. I can almost hear her asking herself:

'How can a woman with such pure creamy white skin have such thoroughly immoral dark thoughts? How can a woman so beautiful on the outside be so heartless and evil on the inside? And why did she select my man? What made her covet him? What made her steal him from me? Why doesn't she feel any guilt about what she's done? What made her corrupt him and make him immoral, like herself? He's like a sex-crazed animal now.

'And what is wrong with me? How have I failed my Marshawn? I work hard. I try to look pretty. I try to be a good lover and a good homemaker. Does he love her just because she's white? Can it be that simple? Please God, tell me it's not that he thinks he's better than me because he has a white girlfriend. Does my husband hate his own race? Please, God, give me answers.'

"So, Bertie, by trying to heal race relations I may have made them worse. I've thought about that possibility. But I've decided to pay it no concern. I've discovered fabulous sex with Marshawn; and I refuse to give that up. I love how we move in rhythm while we make love; especially how he can keep up with me while I rapid-twerk and gyrate. I love how connected we feel when he comes inside me. It's beautiful. When I have a man I want, I refuse to give him back. I play for keeps."

"I can understand your desires, Marty," said a sympathetic Bertie. *"Is that why, when you're having sex with black men, you always tell them you want them to come inside you? I've listened to your film banter with Marshawn and your other orgy partners, Phillip, Stephon, Alvin, and Melvin. You practically begged every one of them to release their ejaculations inside your vagina. I also heard you plead convincingly with another black man named Crawford, the man with that hugely outsized penis. You begged Crawford to come inside you. He finally believed you were serious, and he came inside you. Why? I mean, why is it so important that they ejaculate inside you?"*

"It's the intimacy of it, Bertie. It helps me put all my feelings into the art of copulation. When a man releases his hot cum over my clitoris, it often gives me a fresh orgasm, even if I've had several orgasms before. I'm so highly sensitized to that hot sensation flowing over my clit that I often go off with my partner, simultaneously. Sharing a simultaneous orgasm like that is the ultimate in shared intimacy, don't you agree?"

"Yes, of course it is." Bertie's smile spoke volumes. She had felt the same pleasures Marty was talking about.

"Okay. Well, I especially want my black partners to have that intensely intimate experience with me. It's the ultimate declaration

that we are together, as equals, creating a beautifully artistic film. Urging them to come inside me is the strongest encouragement I can give them to treat me as their equal. It's like my personalized Declaration of Independence or the Constitution. It's letting my black partners know that I truly believe we are equals in all things; especially in our love making."

"Marty, that's so sweet and meaningful. Thank you. Another thing I've noticed, Marty, is your music. You have background music in every seduction scene. Most adult films use a soft jazz theme; but you often use faint strains of religious music as well as soft jazz. Why is that? Is that something you tell your directors you want?"

Usually silent George spoke up: *"Perhaps I can help both of you with this one, since I have taken courses in musicology. Music is primal to humanity. Before speech, fifty thousand years ago, people gathered around campfires to hear one tribal member make sounds on a bone flute, or another person beating out a rhythm on a hollowed-out tree trunk with an animal hide stretched over it. Music draws people closer. It's the primal precursor to talk. It's how feelings were expressed before humans could do exact explanations, make exact demands, or give exact descriptions. Music constantly evolves to reflect and shape feelings. The highest levels of music's emotive powers occur when its rhythms resonate and retain in the brain's amygdule and cerebellum, the regions of emotion and memory.*

"Marty often performs to the Ave Maria and music from the Mass of Saint Cecilia, the Kyrie, the Sanctus, the Gloria, the Credo, and the Agnus Dei. She also selects powerful emotive popular tunes like 'The Rose.' She has evolved her intimacy art to include themes that retain her seduction artistry in her partners' and her viewers' minds. Her music imprints emotive feelings; expressions and memories of every facet of Marty's love making. That music fastens those erotic experiences to their minds, forever. They associate Marty with a goddess-like quality; and that helps cause her viewers to adore her.

"So, whenever one of her fans hears one of those songs, that person associates Marty's sexual performance, frame by frame, with that tune. It rivets the sex scene and the music together and places that union in a special memory. It's a special emotive location that is permanently filed in the viewer's mind. That musical rivet holds that erotic scene in its place, forever. It is recalled whenever the person hears the music; even many years afterwards. It's genius, Bertie. It's pure creative genius. And it's rare. Whether Marty knows why she chose to select those music pieces, or not; choosing them was sheer genius. Her intimate artistry is bound to the primal human need for closeness and shared empathy. Mankind needs that to thrive as a species."

"Let's go with your insight, George." Bertie looked at Marty. Her eyes penetrated now, telling Marty her own genius mind was whirring and clicking. Marty didn't need to wait long.

"*Marty,*" Bertie spoke delicately, deliberately, as was her mental footprint when she was at her creative best: "*When you are in Missionary, when your partner's penis is down stroking into you, I want you to put your mind into a special place. I want to see you smiling broadly, happily during the down strokes of the penis, because I want your mind to be enjoying this delicious subterranean thought:*

'I am relieving my male partner of his unbearable burden of oppression. In my mind, my soul has become the same spiritual soul as Christ's soul in the garden, when he asked the burden of the world's sins to be taken from him; but he was denied. By silence, his father in heaven told him that he was the one chosen to endure the passion of sacrifice. Christ knew he had to surrender his body to his passion for sacrifice, in order to save mankind.'

"Well, Marty, I want you to have that same mindset of blessed acceptance of your role. I want you carrying these thoughts in your mind while you make love with your partner:

'I joyfully accept my calling to help my partner's oppressed soul discover freedom and salvation. I know the old ways that convinced him there was hope have failed him. He no longer has the strength to continue following the old ways. He is with me because he understands his honest reality. His only hope to obtain salvation from tyranny is to surrender to my immoral purity; to love me and accept me in his life; and honor my honest, uninhibited immorality.'

"With those thoughts in your mind, Marty, I want you to inhale deeply while the shaft is going into you on its down stroke; and, I want you to back flex your shoulders to make your breasts lift, pointing your nipple buds heavenward. I also want you to roll your eyes back, until only their whites' show. I want to see heavenly bliss in your facial expression.

"Think. Concentrate. You are living in that divine moment. Your partner is converting his belief system to embrace your passion for immorality. You are overcome. His conversion brings you joy. I want your viewers to subconsciously accept that it's psychologically healthy and normal to take their oppressive stressful burdens to a prostitute; and to LOVE her. By training your thoughts this way, you will communicate the beauty and the goodness of prostitution to your viewers. You will drive more sex workers to advertize their offerings as trailers on your films. Can you have those thoughts while you're on set?"

"Oh, Bertie, absolutely I can. Those are wonderful suggestions. I can do them. Eroticism occurs in the mind. I know what you want. I'll definitely perform all of them."

"Good, Marty. George, would you please partner with Marty a few times on this; with Marty in her Missionary position, until we get the exact expression I'm looking for?"

"My pleasure, Bertie," George nodded he was up for the task.

"Good. Then, Marty, while you are receiving cunnilingus, I also want that same divine smile expression, eyes rolled back, and breasts *thrust outward. And, during straight sex with your male partner, I want to hear you saying words like how beautiful it is; how you can feel the hot semen shooting into you; and how much you love the feeling of that. And with your oral sex partners, I want you saying how beautiful and loving it is and how you want it to continue going on forever; things like that. I don't want to script exact words for you, but I want to hear you talking seductively; expressing joy; and saying what you are feeling at the moment. I'll partner with you for your oral sex practices, until we're capturing the right expressions. Okay? Got it?"*

"Okay, I've got it! I deeply appreciate this, Bertie. Thank you." Marty's nod indicated she was committed to sexual experimentations with Bertie and George in pursuit of becoming the greatest erotic film actress, ever.

"We're going to back up the film now to the beginning of your sequence with Josh again; okay, Marty?"

"Sure, Bertie, what are we looking at?"

"I'm stopping on this section of about a hundred frames where you are holding Josh's penis in your hands. You are stroking it with one hand. Your other hand is massaging his balls and your lips are kissing the top of his penis's head. Do you see what I mean?"

"Yes, I think so."

"Good. Well, that smile on your face; you look so happy; like you're a little girl who has just discovered the Easter Bunny. What were you thinking just then?"

"Oh, gee, Bertie. I was experiencing one of my inner emotional moments just then."

"Tell me. You had such a fascinating look on your face. It came through in the way your eyes shined, too."

"Yes, well, I remember I was just feeling all good and warm inside. I was feeling so thankful that I escaped my grandmother's attempts to drag me into her religious quicksand. I was remembering how she

used to push me to go to religious instruction and services; and how I fought against it. She used to call me on the phone at WEX School and nag me about it."

"That's it? That's all you were thinking?"

"No, that was just the beginning of my thoughts. Those passed rather quickly. Then I was on to thinking how blessed and fortunate I was to be there on that set kissing Josh's marvelous penis. I was thanking my spirit voices for encouraging me to become a prostitute and a porn star. I was silently telling my voices that I was deeply grateful to them for channeling me into prostitution; and how much I loved them for doing that, because I so much loved what I was doing. I just felt warm all over about how I was going to be sucking Josh's splendid penis and making love with him for at least the next hour on that set. I was just so happy for myself. I felt like I was in heaven.

"There's more, Bertie. I also felt that I was doing exactly what my spirits expected of me. I believe the Spirit appeared to Adam and Eve, in the Garden of Eden. Once those two ate of the tree of knowledge; once they understood and knew right from wrong, the Spirit clearly wanted Eve to have urges for Adam. The Spirit wanted the two of them to set the example for the human species. Adam had first rejected all animals as life partners for him, before the Spirit gave him Eve. Eve was given urges for Adam. Well, I try to imagine how Eve must have felt when she first looked upon Adam's penis. I think of myself as being in her same position She must have felt awed:

'Here is a man! He gave me my life from his rib, right? Well, what can I do to answer my natural, Spirit given, urges for my man; and at the same time express to him how profoundly grateful I am to him, for giving up that rib that gave me my life?'

"So, when I'm on set there with Josh, these thoughts arise in my mind: that I'm there to demonstrate to all my viewing fans that it's a

perfectly normal, healthy; even a divinely, godly thing for a woman to express her love and gratitude to her man, by performing fellatio. So, I approach fellatio with a profound sense of divine purpose.

"It's like I know what I'm doing is ordered by divine spirits; and I must do my very best to honor their command to Eve; but really, to all women. And then I tell myself the Spirit would not have me perform fellatio if I wasn't expected to love performing it. That's what helps my mind get into the feelings you see, Bertie. You are seeing how much I truly love sucking penises, especially Josh's."

"Thank you. That helps me a lot. Tell me, Marty, do you have the same feelings when you first have Marshawn's penis in your hands? I mean, do you feel that same sense of gratitude to your spirit and your voices?"

"Yes, absolutely! I know I do. I feel that gratitude to the Spirit and my partner, whenever I first begin to suck an penis. It's like mentally kneeling before an altar for me. I'm just so grateful to be an erotic film artist, making explicit romance scenes; and I try to stay true to my roots; and stay humble and grateful and appreciative about this wonderful career I have."

"Okay, that's very helpful; but is there any sense of difference you feel between when you start sucking Josh's penis, and when you start sucking Marshawn's?"

"Oh, do you mean the racial aspects of it, like me creating explicit erotica scenes with a black man?"

"Well, yes. Do you have different thoughts while you are in those early moments of holding and sucking Marshawn's penis?"

"Now that you've focused me on it; yes, there is a difference. With Marshawn's penis I have those same initial feelings of gratitude to my spirit and voices as I do with Josh's penis. But then this different, new feeling comes over me. It creeps into my limbic zone from my conscious mind, with these deliciously naughty thoughts. I start thinking about how much my handling and sucking Marshawn's

penis is going to drive Aaliyah totally crazy out of her mind. I don't know if you've picked up on that?"

"Actually, I have. You get a whole different sort of gleam in your eyes. It's almost like your face is saying you enjoy being naughty. Is that natural or is it something you are controlling?"

"Oh, Bertie," Marty giggled, *"it's completely spontaneous and natural. In my mind I know I'm crossing Aaliyah's marital boundary. I know I'm driving her crazy. It's that point of departure between her and me. She wants boundaries about what her husband can do with me. But I don't pay attention to boundaries. I don't respect them and I don't respect her. I'm consciously flaunting my disrespect for her; and that makes me that much more focused on teasing the cameras. I'm thinking I want to be as sensuous and naughty as I can possibly be. When I begin kissing the head of Marshawn's penis, I start imagining that Aaliyah will be watching me; and she'll be screaming from mental anguish over what I'm doing with her husband. I know she'll be watching the scene with great apprehension.*

"I put my lips over the head of Marshawn's penis, just enough to cover it down to his circumcision ring. I hold my lips on that ring while my tongue slowly moves back and forth over it. That creates an irresistibly sensuous feeling in his penis. I slowly increase the rapidity of my tongue's back and forth movement until the pleasure sensation I create in his penis becomes impossible for him to bear. I hear Marshawn's breath quicken. He says words like: 'Oh Baby; Oh my God; You're driving me crazy,' things like that. I get the sense that I can make him come into my mouth if I keep doing what I'm doing.

"But I don't want him to come; not just yet. I change the motion of my tongue to a rapid up and down motion over the bottom of his circumcision ring and slightly lower, onto his cock's shaft below its head. I rapidly stroke his shaft with my fingers. I move lower; then rapidly move my tongue back and forth over his balls. And I mouth his balls, one at a time. Marshawn always responds. His breathing

becomes even more rapid. He holds my head in his massive hands. He starts saying romantic things again, like: 'I love you. Oh baby, I totally love you.' Well, I take those words as my cue.

"I want all of him. Even more than his penis, I want his soul. I break off from sucking him and move my face before his. Then I kiss him with a soulful French kiss. Now remember, this is the mouth that has just been sucking and licking his penis. I look lovingly into his eyes and place my hand on his penis. Then, I ask him:

'Do you love me more than you love Aaliyah?' I listen carefully for his reply.

'Yes,' he says.

"I French kiss him again. That's his reward for placing me, a profligate, immoral whore, above his wife. I scour his mouth with my tongue. I'm cleaning his mouth of its memories of her and disconnecting her soul from his. I draw Aaliyah's soul out of him; take it into my mouth; and I swallow it. I ingest it, thereby devouring Aaliyah's essence and her oneness with him. I'm cleansing away all thoughts and feelings that he ever had for her. Then I ask him to confirm what he said:

'Marshawn, you know I am thoroughly immoral. You know I make love with many more men than you. Knowing that about me, can you honestly say you love me? Can you accept me for the uninhibited whore that I am; and not think of me as evil?'

"I again listen for his reply. I pull my head back from his face and carefully study his eyes. Eyes do not lie. This is an important moment for both of us."

'Yes, Marty, I love you. I understand you are immoral; but that doesn't matter to me. I love you with all my heart and soul. I love you more than I have ever loved Aaliyah; and more than I could ever love any other woman.'

"After I heard him say those words, I knew I had captured true love with Marshawn. That is precious, and rare. I felt immensely proud of my bold shamelessness, and of him. I knew then that I was free to love him; cavort openly with him before the entire world; express my thirst for intimacy with him whenever I wished; and wherever he was. I knew I could call him and take him away from Aaliyah, even when he was at home with her; whenever I had urges to make love with him. I knew he was mine. I hugged him. I pressed my body to his. I was slippery hot and wet. I couldn't wait to guide his marvelous penis inside me and meet his thrusts with my own. My mind exploded with lust for intimacy with him."

EATING MILKWEED

"So, you feel naughty, but you don't feel any sort of guilt about what you're doing. Is that right?" Bertie was into her coaching mode: examining, parsing, discerning; ensuring that she had exact understandings of everything that was going on inside her protégé's mind.

"Yes, exactly, I feel no guilt whatsoever. In fact, knowing Marshawn loved me and knowing Aaliyah would be seeing our film helped me deliver those performances as the most explicitly immoral, uninhibited erotic minx I could possibly be. When that feeling within me happens, something instinctive sparks inside me. That enables me to add that extra measure of sinfulness to my performances.

"I imagine myself as a ravenous caterpillar. I need to eat milkweed leaves to grow big and strong, so I can enter chrysalis and transform myself into a butterfly. And when I complete my transformation, I know I'll become the most beautiful, most desirable adult film star in the entire world. I'll be shedding all my old caterpillar ways, which are all my old attachments to religious, moral ways.

"And I will have become completely free of all morality. I'll be a whole new person; purely immoral and free. I'll be like a butterfly; totally carefree. I'll have no concerns about what other people think about me or how they feel about me. They will be like lowly creatures on the ground, below me; and I will flutter over them. And every man in the world will desire to kiss me, and hold me, and make love with me; flutter with me by placing his penis inside my vagina heaven. Men will chase after me; trying to capture me; seeking to sample a taste of my wonderful freedom and my glorious immorality.

"So, while I'm creating a beautiful erotic scene with Marshawn, I feel this added measure of wicked pleasure. I know Aaliyah will see the film. She'll see me making love with Marshawn. So, while I'm on set filming, I know what I'm doing will be driving Aaliyah crazy. And I don't care how she feels. It's because I can forget that she is a wife and mother. Instead, I can think of her as my milkweed. And I am devouring her life, because I must devour her life in order to grow into the top ranks of erotic film stardom. I refuse to stop loving her husband. I won't stop loving him. I can't stop. I couldn't stop loving him if I tried. That would be impossible. I must have him, like a caterpillar must have its milkweed to live."

"But Marshawn and Aaliyah have children. When he holds you and kisses you; when he is ejaculating inside you, while you are feeling his hot cum flowing over your clitoris; or when he's performing cunnilingus and you release an orgasm into his mouth, don't you, even for a few seconds, consider that your affair with him might be hurting their children? Don't you ever have any feelings for those children?"

"No, Bertie, I don't; and I can't. Listen to me. You must see this the way I see it. When I was performing in that orgy scene and Marshawn had just ejaculated inside me, he whispered 'I love you' into my ear. He repeated those words several times. I knew he sincerely meant it. That triggered me. I knew a beautiful man was crying out

to me to help him obtain his freedom from an oppressive situation. I knew he needed me. I knew he wanted me.

"And I took his confession of love as a plea for help. When he said those words a third time, I knew he was telling me the truth. I knew he really did love me. That freed the butterfly spirit that lives within me. Think about that for a minute. Even though I was also doing five other men that afternoon, he could get his mind past that and feel genuine love for me. Not jealousy. It wasn't jealousy. It was honest, genuine love. I knew, right then, that I needed to have an off set, intimate love relationship with him. And I knew a relationship with me would release him from his misery. I knew I would set him free.

"And that relationship, it turned out, required that I destroy his old relationships, which includes the relationship that he had with Aaliyah, and the relationships that he had with his children. That's when this trigger went off inside me. It's when I stopped seeing the people in his old relationships as people. I started seeing them as obstacles that have possessive holds on him. In my mind, they become milkweed leaves which I needed to devour in order to rescue him from his oppression and enable his spirit to have the freedom he craved. And by devouring those milkweed leaves, I became stronger. I grew as a caterpillar grows when it eats milkweed. I grew as a person. My immorality grew. I became more notorious than I was before. In the eyes of my fans and the paparazzi, I became a more beautiful, more wonderous, more desirous erotic film star. I became a magnificent, glorious butterfly."

"So, as Marshawn is inserting his penis into your vagina, you have no concerns about his children; no thoughts about what his penetration into your vagina means for his children; those relationships?"

"No Bertie, none. Honestly none. My vagina is simply devouring some deliciously tender milkweed. My vagina is happily

welcoming his penis and devouring his children's existing lives, too. I believe it is meant to be. And I am loving it. Those moments of penetration make me deliriously happy. Afterwards, I sense the hurts I've caused Aaliyah and the children; and that sense of their hurts increases my joys and pleasure. And I feel proud of what I've done. I've helped Marshawn take another step towards his freedom. And I know that freedom for Aaliyah and the children will naturally follow."

"*Oh Marty, that is so beautiful! I love you so much!*" Bertie held Marty's face in her hands and kissed her.

"*Forgive me for pursuing this line of inquiry, but I needed to understand how dedicated you were to becoming the world's pre-eminent goddess of erotica films. And I just heard how profoundly committed you are to achieving your goal. I visual you as an Olympic Gold Medalist, the very best, most supreme performer in your profession. I know, from my own experiences, how difficult it is to have complete commitment to your goal. And you, my sweetest love, have that. You have the right mindset to excel. I can see that you will never let anything or anyone stand between you and achieving your goal. And I love you so much for being that way. It's a beautiful and rare quality; and you, my darling, have it!*"

"*Thank you, Bertie. You should also know that there's also a psychological component to my compulsion to make love with Marshawn. You see, Aaliyah had a most unfortunate happenstance. That complicated Marshawn's psychology. His love for her was more wrapped up in a sense of cultural duty than honest human love. Her genitals were mutilated when she was a young girl. That's her misfortune. It was the culture she was born ino; what she learned. But, it's not my culture and it's not Marshawn's. He married into it. I don't think he fully understood the long-term ramifications of that kind of marriage and how it would wall off his own emotions. I had no doubts that Marshawn and Aaliyah cared for each other. But that's not the same as passionate, intimate, beautiful bodies enjoying and cherishing each other's intimacy. Marshawn badly needed intimate love. He needed my love.*

"Aaliyah believes that Marshawn must suffer a lack of joy during sex, like the same lack of joy that she suffers. But I believe it's wrong for her to demand that of him, despite their marriage and her culture. When I'm performing fellatio with Marshawn, I feel like I'm doing the work of the spirits; creating erotic love with their fullest blessings. I believe my soul was sent by the Great Spirit of all Living Things to be a thoroughly immoral, intimacy craving lover.

"Spirit promised to never again destroy humans after the Great Flood; but instead, to work with us humans to perfect us. I believe I am one of Spirit's catalysts or change agents, helping Spirit perfect our humanity and our human love; and part of my work is helping Marshawn break away from the barbaric misogynistic cruelty that ensnared unfortunate Aaliyah. So, in a broader sense, I like to think that my vagina is devouring the entire culture which created Aaliyah's lamentable intubation condition. I cannot fathom how a culture regards its women as breeding cattle; not sensitive, loving, relationship partners.

"Her condition is most unfortunate. I cannot imagine not knowing the beautiful pleasures of sexual intercourse. I believe that sexual pleasures; those feelings of intimacy, are the essential recipe for creating human life. I understand how painful it must be for Aaliyah to watch me taking her husband's love away from her, and capturing it for myself.

"But I feel it's my spiritual duty to rescue Marshawn from her regressive way of thinking. I get these dreams and image flashes, where Aaliyah has fallen into this bottomless pit of relentless quicksand. It's drowning her. Her hand has a grasp of Marshawn's foot. She's trying to drag him down with her, into her misery pit. Her face is still visible. It's insisting that her ways are the moral

ways, and my ways are immoral. Therefore, she tells him, he must leave me.

"But I'm there for Marshawn. I'm holding his penis and balls in my hands and I'm sucking him. I'm persuading him that my ways are better. My ways are life's loving ways. I tell Marshawn to hold on to life. I tell him he doesn't have to slide into the horrible inhumane death pit that is submerging his wife. I'm determined not to lose him to the mutilators. I pull him away from his wife. While we make fabulous love, Aaliyah drowns in her quicksand.

"While I suck Marshawn's penis I feel this incredible sense of righteousness, as well as my feelings of love for him; and the same feelings of pure joy I get whenever I perform fellatio. Then, that righteousness feeling brings out yet another feeling. I feel incredibly blessed, and grateful, to be the unapologetic whore that I am; to have the many fabulous career opportunities and door openings that pornography has created for me; and to have my independence, through my film business.

"I shudder to think that if I didn't have my great fortune to be an erotic film star, I might have never been blessed to meet Marshawn. I might never have made love with him. I might never have known the joys of his fabulous penis. That would be a terribly unfortunate travesty; a horrible void in my life. My film work enables Marshawn and me to be shamelessly, madly in love; acting out our love and freely living our explicitly erotic and uninhibited immoral passions, on set, before the entire world. It gives us the freedom to experiment with our love making techniques, for hours upon hours, off set; and license to explain ourselves as striving perfectionists, practicing to perfect our love scenes."

"I see." Bertie felt sobered by Marty's moral philosophizing. Her thoughts turned toward capturing her protégé's passion for immorality, as if she might bottle it. *"That explains the passion I felt while watching your fellatio with Marshawn. Well, then, have you considered this, Marty? Have you thought about creating a film where the theme was a threesome with you, Josh, and Marshawn?"*

"Oh, Bertie, you can read my mind! I have often thought about making that exact film, just me and my two most favorite lovers. Could you arrange that?"

"I'm sure I could. How do think you'd feel while you're making love with both men at the same time?"

"I already KNOW how I'd feel." Marty's heart beat quickened, and her eyes sparkled at the thought of doing a threesome with her two favorite partners.

"I'd feel fabulous times ten, Bertie! I'd be most interested in discovering how my partners feel. I mean when I'm sucking Josh, would that make Marshawn feel jealous? And vice versa? I'm sure I would sense their feelings by the way they make love with me. That would be soooo exciting. Both men already know I love the other. That film would showcase intensely explicit erotica, I'm sure of it. I'd be nympho crazed! Woo, Woo! Choo, Choo! I can't wait to do it! When can we start filming?"

"Well, what do you think of this idea for that film?" Bertie chuckled at Marty's enthusiasm. Her eyes glowed with her vision of the threesome.

"I imagine you lying on your back, on a bed, with your head between their penises. You'll be performing fellatio on both men, alternating between them. I'd like to have almost the entire film focused only on your face; and especially your mouth and lips while you suck their penises. Your hair would never cross your face; so, the explicitness of the erotica aspects of the film would be continuous; completely undisturbed.

"We'd use soft background music, perhaps the 'Ave Maria' that you love so much. If you think you could hold your concentration on both penises long enough to sense their releases and bring them to

simultaneous ejaculations, I'd love to capture that sensational moment on film. I think it would be a spellbinder, with downloads hitting like crazy. What do you think? Do you think you could do that?"

"Oh, Bertie, that's a yes! I KNOW I can do it! Oh, Bertie, yes! A thousand times yes! I absolutely WANT to do it. I'd love making that film. I'd love feeling both men coming simultaneously on my lips and into my mouth. I already know their penises so well; I know my fingers could sense their releases and, by using just the right amount of pressure. I believe I could time their releases perfectly; simultaneously. I'm sure of it. I already know how completely loved I'd feel, knowing both men feel such uninhibited love for me that they could both come into my mouth at the same time.

"While I'm sucking them, I'll imagine I'm obeying the Spirit's commandment to be fruitful and multiply. I'll believe I'm a goddess, coaxing life from both light and darkness. And while they are both coming, it will be all wonderful and good! It will be breathtaking! I'll feel trusted and honored by both men. I want to feel that feeling. That would be the ultimate!

"Perhaps we could title it 'DAYNIGHT CREATION.' We'll win the Fellatio Porn Film of the Year Award for it. How does that sound?"

"I love it, Bertie. I'm certain I can do it. My two favorite lovers; two fabulous penises at the same time! It's never been done before. I love it! I appreciate you so much, Bertie." She hugged Bertie with a monster hug. She kissed Bertie's lips and giggled like a school girl. "I'll work with Josh and Marshawn for weeks, whatever it takes, to get my sucking and stroking coordination and their release timing perfect. I will! You'll see! It will be beautiful. It's a wonderful idea, Bertie."

"Okay, great. I'll make the arrangements right away."

"Wonderful! I'm excited just thinking about it. Thank you. I love you so much, Bertie. Now, my turn. Let me ask some questions."

"Okay, shoot."

"All right. How do you think you'll feel when you see me holding and kissing George's penis the same way I do Josh's and Marshawn's? Would you rather I not do that with George? Would seeing me sucking your husband make you feel possessive and upset with me?"

"Oh, Marty, don't be silly. I'd be very happy for George and very pleased to see you giving fellatio to him. That would prove you have no inhibitions about your relationship with us; and you shouldn't. Whenever you feel the need to indulge your nymphomania or whenever you feel romantic towards George, by all means take his penis into your mouth, or into your vagina, as often and for as long as you please.

"George and I have no marital boundaries about loving you. I'll never erect barriers to you, Marty. I love you. I love you like you're my own daughter; my special blessing. In fact, seeing you doing that with George would make me proud of you, knowing you feel secure in our confidence and love for you. You must feel free to let your sexuality openly express itself, however you wish."

"Thank you for that confidence, Bertie. And, George, how will you feel when you see Bertie and me performing cunnilingus with each other?"

"I'll love it," responded George. *"I'll love watching the two of you and I'll love feeling the love that you two have for each other. I'll love knowing you are both happy. It's beautiful, passionate sex. I hope you enjoy each other, often. I'll be thrilled watching you and Bertie orgasm. The happiness on your faces will make me feel like I'm part of it. I'll love it. Does that help?"*

"Yes, George. You and Bertie are two of my favorite loves. I love both of you."

"Good," Bertie's smiling eyes telegraphed pride in her protégé. *"One more thing, Marty,"* Bertie's eyes narrowed and peered deeply into Marty's, *"I'd like you to tell me if you've ever had any other*

sexual feelings that we haven't talked about here, if you can recall anything, anything at all."

"Gee Bertie; I think we've covered everything." Marty shrugged her shoulders. But then she looked deeply into Bertie's eyes and saw a trusted friend, someone she could share her darkest secret with.

RUSH FEELING

"Well, wait; there is one other feeling I have had. It's a deliciously wrong feeling. I know it's terribly wrong, but it was incredibly beautiful; spiritually, divinely out of this world beautiful. It gave me a blood rush, unlike anything else ever has, before or since."

"What was it, Marty?" Bertie's head lifted and cocked to question her student. *"Describe it for me, please. I'll try to work it into your films."*

"I don't know if I should, Bertie; and I don't think we could ever capture that feeling on film." Marty's eyes searched the floor for her thoughts.

"I shouldn't have seen what I saw that made me feel that way," Marty said haltingly. *"If I share this secret with you, you must promise me you'll keep it totally confidential. You must never tell another soul, okay?"*

"Of course, my sweet baby. Of course." Bertie reached out her hand and placed it upon Marty's shoulder. Her warm eyes looked with reassuring understanding and trust into Marty's. *"Everyone needs someone they can trust with a secret. Anything you tell me will be strictly confidential. I promise."*

"Okay," Marty's eyes spanned the age difference as they searched Bertie's. Her look begged Bertie to understand. *"I will tell you. I witnessed a man being murdered. At first, I thought what was happening was terrible. But then, the longer I watched the murder taking place, the more I realized I was observing something*

beautiful. A wild erotic feeling overwhelmed me. Suddenly, I desperately needed sex. It was as if life itself depended upon me. I began kissing and sucking two penises, and making love. I don't understand how seeing a murder affected me that way, but it did.

"Maybe my body somehow felt called to procreate and replace the life that was taken. I'm not sure. But I was on the pill, so I knew I couldn't get pregnant. So, it wasn't me feeling some need to create a baby. It was more of a bodily urge; a sudden happening; a desperate need to fornicate. Something primal released inside me. It overwhelmed me. I felt that murder was somehow good; like it was a necessary part of life's rituals. I couldn't help feeling the way I felt. I felt sensational inside; glorious to be alive.

"My heart began pounding. I had this deep yearning in my breast. I internally celebrated the ultimate immoral deed; seeing it happen in that expressive, real way. By not trying to stop it, I knew I was also immoral. But my inner thrill honored that act of murder. It felt glorious; a different kind of thrill; so meaningful!

"That thrill became lightning, flashing through my blood. Nothing else before had ever turned me on like that. My soul became immoral. I knew if I made love immediately after that murder, I would become part of that gloriously immoral scene; and that life altering scene would become me. And my mind, all my senses, needed to capture the magnificent beauty of that scene. I can't explain it. It must have been the way the ancient pagans felt when they sacrificed someone. I don't know what made me feel the way I did. But whatever it was, I knew I had to make love; absolutely had to; with wild abandon. And I did. I had sensational love making. I'll never forget it."

'Oh my God!' Miss Iniquity intervened. Her voice screamed into Marty's mind, trying to bring her back to her senses. *'What have you just done? You've spilled the beans! How could you be so stupid? You are stupid, stupid, STUPID! Now Bertie knows you've witnessed a murder! And, Stupid, YOU were the murderess, weren't*

you? It was that one where the guy got off the table; and you ran him down and stabbed him thirty times; and the entire time you were stabbing him, you were sparking inside; getting more and more juiced. And the strobe light was making you more excited and closer to having your orgasm. Wasn't that the one?'

'Yes, Iniquity,' Marty's mind answered her voice. *'That's the murder.'*

'Well, girl, you'd better do immediate damage control. Tell Bertie, right this minute, that your memory is a little hazy; and you don't want to talk about this anymore, ever again. Tell her it troubles you to bring up that feeling; and tell her you want her to just let it go.'

'Okay, yes, Miss Iniquity. I'm sorry. It won't happen again.'

"Bertie, George," whispered Marty hoarsely, *"I'm actually not sure about what I saw that day and I'd like to forget it. I think maybe I was just having a bad dream. I was having a lot of headaches for a while, back then. It might have been a hydration issue. I'm not sure why I had crazy thoughts like that. Please forget I said those words. They just came out; but they weren't really me talking. I just have weird dreams, sometimes. Let's never talk about it again, okay?"*

"Okay my darling, whatever you say. We have enough material to work with without that anyway. I'll never say a word about this to anyone, I promise you. I've already forgotten I ever heard it." Bertie shrugged her shoulders and smiled to Marty her most benevolent, motherly smile.

"I haven't heard a thing," said George, shrugging his shoulders and slowly shaking his head.

But, in the back of Bertie's mind she knew the three of them now shared a profound secret. It would bind them more closely together than their film craft or any amount of money ever could.

More to come.

What was Marty thinking? Why did she reveal to Bertie that she'd witnessed a murder? Bertie promises she'll keep that reveal confidential. But can Marty trust her to keep a secret like that? Will Marty tell David about this reveal; and, if she does, how might David receive that information?

In BUTTERFLY TRADECRAFT, our sixth book of THE SECRET BUTTERFLY SERIES™, we'll discover some closely held secrets that Bertie employs to create Marty's most successful erotic films, ever. Gwendolyn, a wealthy benefactor of Marty's makes her appearance in our next segment. Gwen will reveal a fascinating side of herself that no one except Bertie fully understands. We'll discover how deeply Bertie feels about her long-time friend.

Unknowingly, Marty could have placed David in an impossible double conundrum. In the final chapter of BUTTERFLY TRADE-CRAFT, our sixth book of the Series, Poon, the innocent Monarch butterfly decides she must ponder everything she hears. She prays to the Great Spirit of All Living Things for guidance before she journeys onward in search of Tang. As a butterfly, Poon doesn't understand murder. She can't imagine it happening in her Butterfly World. She understands that her prayers are urgent. She knows she faces a formidable challenge. She must find the strength to flutter across a vast ocean before she can mate above the canopy of the Mexican jungle. She feels an overpowering internal urge. Her instincts tell her it is the whole reason for her having a life. She must mate with Tang.

Come flutter along with me, Melanie Monarch, as I narrate BUTTERFLY TRADECRAFT, the riveting sixth book of THE SECRET BUTTERFLY ™ SERIES.